DEATH WATCH

DEATH WATCH

THE SILENCER SERIES
BOOK 21

MIKE RYAN

Cover Design: The Cover Collection

1

Recker was sitting on the bench in the park, waiting for his girlfriend to arrive. It was a beautiful, sunny day. He watched a few kids run by him, parents pushing their children in strollers, and a few people running by as they jogged. It was one of those moments where he let doubt creep into his mind about what he did. One of those times when maybe he wanted a more normal life. Those thoughts were quickly erased once he saw Mia walking toward him.

Recker stood up, giving his girlfriend a kiss as she got near him. She had a bag in hand, and handed him a sandwich as she sat down.

"Nothing like a beautiful day in the park having lunch."

Recker looked up at the sky. "Yeah, it's a peaceful feeling, isn't it?"

"So how are things at work?"

"Oh, you know, the usual."

"Anything pressing?"

Recker stopped chewing on his sandwich for a second. She rarely asked about his work. And when she did, she never asked if anything was pressing. But, he let it go and continued chewing.

"No, nothing too pressing. Why?"

"Oh, no reason. Just wondering."

Recker nodded, knowing there was a reason. But he was willing to wait for what it was. They continued with some small talk, along with eating, for a little while longer.

"Days like this make me not want to go back to work," Mia said.

"This kind of weather will make you want to skip work for sure."

"So how's David?"

Recker froze for a second, then slightly turned his head toward her to look at her for a second. He knew something was coming. He didn't know what. But something was coming.

"Uh, David's fine. You did just see him two or three days ago."

"Yeah, but that was at the office. I didn't know if anything had come up since then to stress him out or anything."

"Things are always stressing him out. You know that."

"Yeah. Right. What about Chris?"

Now Recker turned his head fully to stare at her.

Mia looked at him, as well, feeling his stare. "What?"

"We just had dinner with him last night. You know how he is."

"Oh, yeah." Mia chuckled. "That's right. I forgot."

"Stressful day for you?"

"Hmm? What?"

"You seem kind of forgetful at the moment. Or preoccupied. Everything good?"

"Oh. Yeah. I mean, mostly. For the most part. I guess."

Recker turned his head in the opposite direction, scratching the back of his head. He had a smirk on his face, knowing Mia had something on her mind that she didn't want to reveal. At least not yet. Instead of letting her twist in the wind for a while, Recker thought he'd help move things along.

"So what'd you wanna ask me?"

"Huh? What do you mean?"

"There's clearly something on your mind," Recker said. "Why don't you just come out with it?"

"There's nothing really on my mind."

"Really?"

She finished off her sandwich and shook her head. "Nope."

Recker waved his hand in the air. "OK."

"Well, I guess maybe there is something."

Recker let out a laugh as he looked at the ground.

"You don't have to be that secretive about it. Just come out with it."

"It's kind of about work, and kind of not. It's... and I really don't even want to bother you with it, except it's... it's this kind of thing that's..."

Recker smiled and put his hand on her knee. "Mia, it's fine. Talk to me. What's going on?"

"There's this security guard at the hospital. His name is Frank. He's been there a long time. He's probably close to retirement, I think. Another year or two, I'd imagine. Anyway, he's always there. I don't ever remember not seeing him. You know, unless he had a day off or something."

"Yeah?"

"Anyway, he hasn't shown up to work for a few days. It's going around the hospital."

"What is?" Recker asked.

"Rumors. About what's going on."

"Which is what?"

"That's the thing. Nobody knows."

"Maybe he's got things going on. Called out for a few days."

Mia shook his head. "He hasn't, though. I was talking to one of the other guards yesterday, and nobody there knows anything either. But he said Frank didn't call out. He just stopped showing up."

"I'm sure there's a reason."

"That's the reason we're afraid of."

"What?"

"We're afraid something happened to him."

"Such as?" Recker asked.

Mia shrugged. "I don't know. Whatever happens to people. You probably have more experience with that than me."

"Anybody tried calling him?"

"Of course. Doesn't answer his phone. Someone even went to his apartment to check on him. No answer."

Recker rubbed his nose as he tried to think of an alternative answer. He didn't have one at the moment.

"This isn't some young kid who's getting pulled in ten different directions with life choices. We're talking about a guy in his late sixties. All he had was his work. The people at the hospital were like a second family to him. He wouldn't just blow it off."

"You're sure of that?"

"Yes."

"Maybe he had a medical emergency and got admitted to a different hospital."

Mia shook her head. "No. That's not it. I'm sure of it."

"So you think something happened to him?"

"I don't know what to think. I don't want to think that."

"Is this your way of asking me to look into this?"

Mia sheepishly smiled. "Well, I mean, if you're not busy or anything and you have the time. I don't want to force you or anything, and you certainly don't have to. But…"

"Mia, it's fine. I've got the time. If it's important to you, I can look into it."

She leaned over and kissed him. "Thank you."

"I'll probably need everything you know about him. As much as you can."

"I was thinking maybe you could talk to his supervisor at work? He's got all that."

"OK. I guess I can do that."

"Do you have time now?"

Recker raised an eyebrow. "Mia, did you already tell this person that I would talk to him?"

"What? No! No, definitely not. No way. I wouldn't do that, especially without knowing exactly what else you were involved with at the moment."

"Maybe implied?"

"Well, you know, I just said that maybe you'd be available. Just maybe. No guarantees or promises or anything. I just kind of… mentioned that you might be… available?"

Mia crinkled her nose as she said it, hoping that her boyfriend wouldn't be mad. But Recker couldn't help but smile.

"Does this guy know anything about me?" Recker asked.

"No. I just told him that you worked in private security and that your team specialized in things like this. That's all."

Recker took a deep breath. "OK. I'll go talk to this guy."

"Oh, thank you!"

She almost jumped on top of him to give him a hug.

"Do you think the guys would mind you looking in on this?"

Recker shook his head. "These are the things that we do. And when it comes to people we know, that's something that goes to the top of the list. You know they won't."

"I don't know why I was nervous about asking you."

"I don't know either. You know I've always been willing to help anyone that had a problem. Especially if it's you."

"I guess I just didn't want to drag you away from something important."

"This is important. If this guy went missing, we need to figure out why. And we will. Promise."

2

___

On the way back to the hospital, Mia called Frank's supervisor, letting him know when they were going to get there. He agreed to meet them in the cafeteria when they arrived. When Recker and Mia got there, she spotted the man and pointed him out. They walked over to the table and sat down across from him.

"Hi, Joe," Mia said.

"Hey. Thanks for coming."

"This is Mike."

Recker and Joe shook hands.

"So you're in security too, huh?"

Recker smirked. "In a way."

"Thanks for looking into this for us. We really appreciate it."

"What can you tell me about Frank? Mia went over the basics, but did you notice anything different about him lately? Anything bothering him? Acting unusual?"

Joe shook his head and lifted his hands up emphatically. "No! No, not at all. That's what's so crazy about this. He seemed normal. Just like he always is."

"How long has he actually been missing?"

"Well, he hasn't shown up for his last four shifts. And he had one day off in the middle of them. So it's been about five days now. It's totally unlike him. I don't know if Mia mentioned it, but the guy hasn't missed a day of work in ten years. Even last year, he had the flu for a few days. He came right in on time. Of course, I sent him home early to get better and all, but that's the kind of guy Frank is. He comes in, sick or not, no matter what. Nothing slows him down. That's why it's so alarming that he just no-shows like this. It's not like him."

"What about the police?" Recker asked. "Contact them?"

"Yeah, after about three days. They said they'd look in on it and all, but I contacted them this morning, just to get an update on their progress."

"And?"

"Didn't have any progress to report. Said they checked his place, found no signs of struggle. Doesn't look like he'd been there in a few days. They don't know. They'll keep looking, so they say, but we both know how that goes. Other cases come up, things with no leads get shoved to the background, and before you know it, a year will go by or something. I don't want Frank to get lost. He's a good man. He deserves better than just a file at the bottom of someone's desk."

Recker nodded, understanding the concern. "What about family?"

"None, really. Frank's wife died close to ten years ago. As a matter of fact, that might have been when he last took a day off that wasn't scheduled. Maybe that's why he's been so dedicated. The job, the people here, it's really all he's got. It's like a family to him."

"What about kids?"

"I know he had a daughter. He doesn't talk much about her, though. She's grown, married, moved out to California, I think. I know he doesn't see her much, or if he does at all. Whether they're close or not, my instincts say no, but I'm not sure."

"Why do you not think they're close?"

"Like I said, never talked about her much. Maybe in passing here or there, but you know, most parents talk about the achievements of their kids, what they're up to, grandkids, stuff like that. But Frank never really did. In the last year, I think he might have mentioned his daughter once or twice. That's it. Just seemed to me that they weren't close. But I could be wrong on that. It was just an impression."

"I can check on that. No problems with anyone here or anything?"

"Nah. Everybody loved Frank. He always made it a point to talk to people here. Get to know them. Even if he only saw them once a month. The younger people working here always loved seeing him. He was like a second dad or grandfather, you know? An easy-going guy you could talk to, even if you didn't know him all that well."

"So not an enemy in the world?"

"Pfft. I don't know who it could be, if he had one. If you didn't like Frank, there's something wrong with you. Ain't no other way around it. He's as good a guy as there is."

"OK. I'll need everything you have on him. Address, phone number, anyone he hung out with outside of work, email, everything you got."

"Already figured you would," Joe said. He reached into his shirt pocket and removed a folded piece of paper. He unfolded it and handed it to Recker. "I anticipated the question. This is everything I know about him."

Recker read what was on it and was satisfied. It had the basics that he needed. It would be enough to get started.

"Was he dealing with any medical problems that you know of?"

"Never mentioned anything," Joe answered. "Never saw him taking any pills either. If he was on something, he never let on."

Recker let out a sigh as he rubbed his forehead, continuing to look at the paper in front of him. It certainly didn't add up. Why would a guy who seemed to be universally loved wind up disappearing? Unless he was in one of those wrong place, wrong time types of deals.

One thing that did get Recker's attention was Frank's address. He'd been there before. Not at Frank's specific apartment, but he'd been in that area. It wasn't noted as one of the best. Recker wondered if maybe Frank had gotten caught up in something. Something he obviously wasn't supposed to. But then again, considering everything he'd been told so far, it didn't seem like Frank would be the type of guy who'd get mixed up in something, unless it was an accident. But, at this point, everything was pure speculation. Oftentimes, that didn't add up to much.

They continued talking for a little while longer, with Recker trying to get as much information as he could on Frank. Everyone had their own little quirks and idiosyncrasies. Maybe one of them would give Recker a clue on what happened. But once Recker had everything Joe could give him, it was time to go to work.

"I guess that's it, huh?"

"For now," Recker replied.

"Will you keep me updated?"

"I can do that."

Recker took a business card out of his pocket and handed it to Joe. It was a plain white card with a phone number on it.

"What's this?"

"If you have anything else, something you forgot, something you find out, you call me there."

"Don't like to advertise much, huh?"

Recker grinned. "We like to operate on a... smaller scale."

"Yeah, so, I guess that's it?" Joe stood up and shook Recker's hand. "I really appreciate you looking into this."

"Glad to do it. Hope we can find something."

Joe walked away from the table. Recker continued staring at the paper that he'd been given with all of Frank's information on it.

"What is it?" Mia asked. "You look troubled by something."

Recker glanced at her and shook his head. "No, it's... not that. It's nothing in particular. It's just always troubling when someone mysteriously vanishes."

"You don't think that...?"

"Right now, I don't think anything. And neither should you. Definitely don't think the worst."

"What else can there be?"

"There can be quite a bit," Recker replied. "Maybe there was an emergency with his daughter in California. Maybe he fell and hit his head, was taken to a different hospital, and has temporary amnesia. There are all sorts of things."

"But none of them likely."

"Who's to say what's likely? All I'm saying is don't

lose hope. Until the light's been extinguished, keep the fire burning."

"When did you get all psychological?"

"It's the new me."

Mia kissed him on the cheek. "I like it. But I gotta get back to work too. Do you need anything else?"

"Nope. I'm good."

"All right. I'll see you later tonight, then."

As soon as Mia left, Recker took out his phone to call Jones.

"Hey, need you to start running some information down."

"Taking cases without me, are you?" Jones asked.

"Sometimes I just hang a shingle out on the corner. Get whatever business I can. Especially when you don't have anything."

"Should I just start creating problems out of thin air?"

"Not necessary when I start getting the jobs for us."

"Indeed. And how did you catch this one?"

"Security guard at the hospital Mia works. He's gone missing. Mia's pretty worried. Just talked to his boss, too. They're all pretty shaken up about him."

"Oh. Well what do you have? I'll get started on it."

Recker read off everything that was on the paper that Joe gave him.

"That should be enough to work on," Jones said. "I assume I'll see you in a little bit?"

"Not just yet. While I'm out, I figure I'll head over to

this guy's apartment. See if I can dig something up. I'll swing by Chris' place and pick him up to give me some backup."

Jones' ears perked up. "Backup? Are you already expecting trouble?"

"Expecting? No. But Frank's apartment isn't exactly in the greatest of neighborhoods. I'd rather have him there just in case."

"Should I inform him you're coming?"

"No, you've already got your hands full. Just get started on all that other stuff."

"All right," Jones said. "Let me know if you need anything else."

Once Recker hung up, he immediately called his other partner.

"Don't tell me," Haley said.

"Don't tell you what?"

"You need me for something?"

"Well, I mean, you don't have to."

"This is my first day off of the week, you know."

"Oh. Um, well, like I said, you don't have to. It shouldn't take more than an hour or two."

Haley loudly sighed into the phone. "All right. What are we into?"

"Just checking out an apartment."

"And I just got all lathered up, too."

Recker raised an eyebrow. "Uh, am I interrupting something?"

"Well, I just got all lotioned up, laying outside in the courtyard with my speedo on. Working on my tan."

Recker was silent for a moment.

"You still there?" Haley asked.

"Yeah, I guess. I'm not sure what to say now."

Haley laughed. "You want a picture?"

"No! Please tell me you're joking."

"No, why would I be joking?"

"Uh. I don't know." Recker shook his head, trying to jar the images out of his mind. "Now I lost my train of thought."

Haley continued laughing. "Good. That's what you get."

"Say what?"

"If I have to work on my day off, you get visions burned into your head that you can't shake loose. Now we're even."

Recker chuckled. "I'm not sure that's a fair trade."

"Maybe not. But that's your problem."

"You're not really sitting there like that, are you?"

"No, I'm just sitting here watching a show. Figured if I had to work, you'd get the worst end of it."

"You know, if you really want the time off, I can go alone. It's no problem."

"No, it's good," Haley said. "I don't really mind. David finally came up with something for us?"

"No, this is from Mia. Security guard at her hospital's gone missing. By all accounts, very out of character. Figured we had the time to check it out."

"Works for me."

"I'll come by your place and pick you up."

"I'll be ready. What do you think we got here?"

"I don't know," Recker answered. "But one thing's for sure, isn't it? People don't disappear for no reason. And I have a feeling when we find out the reason here, we won't like what we find."

3

Recker and Haley pulled into the parking lot of the apartment complex that Frank lived in. As soon as they found a spot, they observed a drug deal going down at the corner of the building. Right out in the open, not really a care in the world. Recker sighed. He'd been there before, so he knew there was quite a bit of criminal activity there, but it always made him shake his head when it was done so openly.

Recker and Haley sat there for a few minutes, just observing their surroundings. Since they had been there before, they knew things could get hairy quickly. They had to be cautious. The residents there, and the whole area, really, didn't take too kindly to strangers. If you weren't known and were visiting there, people assumed you were either with the police, undercover, or were looking to start trouble. Either case could be troubling for Recker.

"What's his number again?" Haley asked.

Recker looked at his phone. "B9."

Haley pointed to his right. "Over that way."

There were numerous buildings, but none of them were connected, though all were very close together. They observed a couple known gang members walk past one of the buildings.

"This should be fun," Haley said.

Recker smirked. He knew his partner was being facetious, but there were very few things in their line of work they could call fun. This certainly wasn't one of them.

"We could just wait until after dark."

"I'm not sure it makes much difference," Recker replied.

"They can see us better in the daytime."

"But there will be more out and about after the sun goes down."

"That's true."

They kept their eyes on the gang members until they disappeared out of sight. The coast was clear for the moment.

"I say we go now," Recker said.

"Yeah, let's do it."

They got out of their car and swiftly walked over to the B building. They kept turning their heads, looking for any sign of trouble as they walked over there. Thankfully, they reached it without a problem.

Once inside, they instantly came across a man

walking past them. He gave them a strange glance. They definitely looked out of place there. They kept moving, though, eventually passing a woman, who also looked at them curiously. No one said a word, though.

They finally reached Frank's apartment. They stood just outside the door. Just as Haley was about to fiddle with the lock, the neighboring apartment door opened. A middle-aged man stepped out.

"What you guys doin'?"

Recker turned his head. "What does it look like we're doing? We're going into this apartment."

"That don't belong to you."

"We're investigating something."

"Oh. You cops?"

"Do we look like cops?"

The man sized them up for a second. "Well, yeah, kind of."

"Well there you go."

"You got badges?"

"We don't have time for this," Recker said. "We're not here for you. Get back in your apartment and let us do this."

"All right, all right, just calm down there. Jeez, you're just like the other guys."

"What other guys?"

"Those other cops that were here. They didn't want nothing to do with me either."

"Why should they?"

The man shrugged. "Well, when you try and help them out with stuff, think you got information for them, and they just push you along cause they got better things to do, apparently, it gets a little off-putting, you know?"

"You had information for them?"

The man threw his hands up. "They didn't wanna hear it. Just pushed me along, told me to get back inside, and never heard from them again. It's just like everything else around here."

"What do you mean by that?" Recker asked.

"Police, man. They always say they wanna help, get things cleaned up and all, but you never see or hear from them. People around here want the scum and riff-raffs out of here." The man shrugged again. "But nothing ever changes."

"Maybe we can do something about that."

The man looked past Recker, seeing Haley on one knee, appearing like a burglar trying to pick the lock.

"Why's he doing that, man?"

Recker looked back at his partner. "The other guys lost the key, if you can believe it."

The man put his hands up to his shoulders. "Man, I can believe just about anything. A lot of incompetence out there these days. In all professions. I guess it's no different with you guys."

"Apparently so."

"I mean, I can get you in if you want."

"You got a key?"

"Yeah." He reached into his pocket.

"Why do you have a key to Frank's apartment?"

"Me and Frank kind of looked after each other. Got to around here. Need someone to have your back, you know? And we had a lot in common. There was a twenty-something year age difference between us, but we liked a lot of the same things. He was good people."

"Why do you say 'was'?"

"He's missing, ain't he? Around here, we all know what that means. Especially with Frank. He wouldn't just up and leave."

Recker pointed with his thumb toward the door. "Can you open that?"

"On one condition."

"What's that?"

"You let me go in there with you. I can let you know if something's missing or ain't right in there."

"You've been in there before?" Recker asked.

"Oh yeah. Many times. One of the things we had in common was chess. We used to play each other two or three times a week."

Recker grinned and nodded. "Open it up. What's your name, by the way?"

"Jamar."

Haley got up and moved out of the way as Jamar stuck his key in and opened the door. Haley walked in first, followed by Recker. Jamar snuck in behind them.

"Just don't touch anything," Recker said.

As Haley started the search, Recker had more questions for their new friend.

"You said you had information for the other cops that were here. What was it?"

Jamar put his hand on his forehead and looked down. "I dunno, man. A couple days before Frank disappeared, I heard him talking to someone. Well, I say talking. It was more like yelling."

"Do you know who he was talking to?"

Jamar shook his head. "No idea. And I don't know if it was someone in his apartment or if he was on the phone, but it was loud. I mean, it was coming through my walls pretty good. Walls in these buildings ain't too thick, you know?"

"What did you hear?"

Jamar grimaced. "Ah, you know, I don't try to listen in to other people's conversations, you know? But it was so loud, I couldn't help but hear a few things. Frank kept saying something like, 'I've always tried to help you', or 'I've done nothing but try to be there for you', things like that. Kept repeating that over and over a few times. Really strange."

"And you don't know who he was talking to?"

"No idea."

"Didn't ask him?"

"Nah. Man's personal things are his own business. Not for me to interfere or nothin', unless he asks for an opinion or something, you know?"

"I get it," Recker said.

"Like I said, it was really strange. I ain't never heard Frank raise his voice like that. Not even close. I mean, he was agitated. Like I ain't never heard him agitated before."

"You didn't hear him say a name or anything?"

"No, I don't think so. Like I said, I didn't want to listen in to his private stuff, you know? I just cranked the TV up a little, watched the Sixers, tried to block it out and all."

"How long did it go on for?"

"It was only a couple minutes. And to be honest, watching the Sixers, I got a little distracted myself, you know? I started getting all hot and bothered once they bricked a few three's, you know?"

Recker smirked. "I hear you. Not their best year, is it?"

Jamar puffed. "Man, you ain't kidding. Their bench is awful, and they need a backup point guard in the worst way. And somebody teach these people to shoot some free throws, you know what I'm saying? I mean, they're shooting something like sixty or seventy percent from the line. Those are free points!"

"Maybe next year."

"It's always next year. Pretty soon a decade's past and it's the same thing. Maybe next year. I'm tired of next year, you know?"

"I hear ya. Back to Frank..."

"Oh, yeah, anyway, I ain't never heard him yell like that to anybody. And I've been here eight years. Never heard him raise his voice or say a mean word to nobody. Still hard to believe he's gone."

"Did he have a lot of visitors?" Recker asked.

"Nah, not really. Maybe a friend or two from the building, but nobody really from outside. He kept to himself mostly when he was here. And not too many people want to visit here, you know? This place has been going downhill for a few years now."

"Why do you guys stay?"

"It's home. It's hard to leave your home. Plus, who's to say you won't move somewhere else and it won't be just as bad? Crime's everywhere. Well, you know. Don't have to tell you."

"Unfortunately, I do."

Recker and Jamar started looking around, joining Haley in their search of the rooms.

"Let me know if you see something out of place or missing," Recker said.

After looking for a while, they didn't see anything that didn't look like it belonged. They didn't uncover any documents that gave them a clue, or any strange items that would lead them in another direction.

"You see anything that looks like it's missing?" Recker asked.

Jamar crossed his arms, his eyes scanning the room. "Nah. Not a thing. Doesn't look like..." He stopped mid-sentence as he looked at the bookcase along the far wall.

Recker noticed his demeanor. "You see something?"

Jamar walked over to the bookcase. It appeared as if he were looking for something in particular.

"What is it?"

Jamar stretched out both his arms toward the bookcase. "There used to be a box. Right here." He pointed to the third shelf from the bottom. "Right on this shelf."

"What kind of box?"

"Ah, you know, just a box. Like, uh, one of those jewelry type boxes, you know? About, so big." He demonstrated the size with his hands. "You know the ones. You put jewelry or important papers, things like that."

"What was inside?"

"No idea. I never looked inside. Not my business. But I remember it was here."

"Why would that go missing?" Recker asked, mostly talking to himself.

"Can't say. And he kept it locked, I know that."

"How?"

"One time he showed me a picture of his daughter in there. And he had to take out a key to open it."

"When's the last time you saw it?" Haley asked.

"Oh, must've been last week or so. Yeah, I think that was it. Definitely was there a week or two ago. I remember that much."

"Must've had something valuable in there."

"Yeah, I noticed other things in there when he took out the picture, but didn't really see what it all was. Could've been other papers, or stamps, or maybe old valuable baseball cards, you know? I just don't know."

"We noticed some gang members hanging around outside," Recker said. "Frank ever have any problems with them?"

"Never any heated conversations or anything. But if they were hanging around, messing with someone, Frank wouldn't hesitate to tell them to leave a kid alone, or peddle their drugs elsewhere, things like that. And sometimes they listened, and sometimes they brushed him off."

"Think maybe they could've done something to him?"

Jamar shrugged. "Who knows? These days, I wouldn't put nothing past nobody."

They took another look around the apartment, but didn't notice anything else besides the missing jewelry box.

"I think that's all we're gonna get here," Haley said.

"Yeah," Recker replied. "I think you're right."

"At least we know about the jewelry box."

"But no way of knowing what was in it."

"Hey, before you guys go, I gotta know something," Jamar said. "Can I ask? And if it ain't the truth, you don't gotta worry about me or nothing, I know how to keep my mouth shut."

"Go ahead."

"Are you guys really cops?"

Recker briefly glanced at his partner. Jamar didn't seem like the type of guy who'd give them a problem. And it really didn't matter if he would. They'd be gone by the time that would happen.

"No."

"I didn't think so," Jamar said. He put his hands up. "You ain't gotta worry about me. I won't say nothing."

"Put your hands down. You don't need to fear us."

"Who are you guys? Really."

Recker reached into his pocket and removed one of his business cards. He handed it to Jamar.

"It's just a phone number."

"I don't usually like to advertise my presence," Recker said. "But if you ever need me for something around here, you can call it. I'll be around."

"Who do I ask for?"

"The Silencer."

Jamar's eyes almost popped out of his head upon hearing the name. "No way. You're him?"

"Last I checked."

"I've heard of you. I've heard you're one of the good ones."

"I try."

"If you're on Frank's case, I feel much better about it. How'd you get on this?"

"Somebody who knows Frank at the hospital just happens to know me. Thought I might want to check it out."

"Well God bless them, man. Cause now, like I said, I'm feeling better knowing you're on this."

Recker pointed to the card. "If you ever need anything, you call that, all right? I'll be here."

"It's good knowing I got this in my back pocket. Especially with Frank being gone, it don't feel the same around here. What if I'm next or something?"

"Like I said, you call that."

Jamar stuck his hand out to shake, which Recker obliged.

"Appreciate this," Jamar said. "Hopefully I won't need this, but I have a feeling, somehow, I will."

Recker didn't respond, but he had a similar feeling. He didn't think of it before, but what if Jamar knew more than he was saying? Maybe he didn't know himself. But if Frank went missing, was there a chance that Jamar might find himself in a similar situation? It was tough to say without more useful information. But as Recker looked at Jamar, he got the feeling he'd be seeing him again too. And probably soon.

4

Recker and Haley walked out of the apartment, ready to call Jones with their findings, as well as seeing if he had come up with something on his end. Recker never got the phone out of his pocket, though. As soon as they stepped outside, they looked over to their car and saw a few unfamiliar faces hanging around it.

Haley nudged his partner in the arm. "Looks like we got company."

"I see them."

They counted five. Three were leaning up against the hood, while the other two were on each side. They appeared to just be lounging, probably waiting for them to return.

"How you wanna play this?"

"Let's try the easy way first," Recker answered.

"And if that doesn't work?"

"One way or another, they're leaving."

Recker and Haley made their way to their car, stopping just short of it.

"Something we can help you guys with?" Recker asked.

A man with a red durag on spoke up, looking and acting like the leader of the group. "Uh, yeah, man, you can tell us what you were doing in there."

"That's not your business."

"Everything around here is my business."

"Oh, are you in charge around here?"

"That's right. And nobody comes in here that I don't know, or know what they're doing. And that includes you."

"Well, I guess you'll just have to accept it differently this time."

The man pushed himself away from the car, looking like he was egging for a fight. He took a few chews of his gum as he looked at Recker and Haley.

"Think you guys are bigshots or something? You can just roll in here, do what you want, then leave without nobody saying a word?"

"That's exactly what we're gonna do," Recker replied. "We don't answer to you. And there's nothing you can do to stop us. So unless you have a strong interest in visiting the hospital to get your jaw wired shut, I'd suggest you step away from our car and go hassle some elderly people crossing the street. From the looks of you guys, that's probably about all you're good for."

One of the other men pushed himself away from the hood, looking like he wanted to tangle with Recker, though the leader put his arm out to prevent him from going any further.

"I know you guys probably thrive on intimidation and fear, but you don't scare us," Recker said.

"We should."

"Should be the other way around. You should be fearing us."

"Now why would we do that? I only got a high school degree, but I can count pretty good. Looks like it's five against two right now. Unless I got my math wrong?"

"Your math is right. But the odds are wrong."

"The odds?"

"They're in our favor. You don't have enough to handle us."

The man laughed. "Oh, is that right? You two boys are gonna throw down with us and just knock us all off, huh?"

Recker grinned. "Yeah. That's right."

"I almost would like to see it."

"Make a move and you will."

One of the other men spoke up. "Yo, T, let's just take these guys out and move on, man. What are we fooling around for?"

"Probably because T is smarter than you," Recker

said. "He's probably standing there wondering why the two guys in front of them are not intimidated or afraid like everyone else is. That probably gets him thinking, saying, 'what is it about them that I don't know'? Why are they not scared? Do they have something up their sleeve? Or maybe they're just the two baddest mofo's we've ever come across." Recker then pointed at the other man. "And see, that's the thing. You really don't know what you're going up against right now, do you?"

T licked his lips, appearing like he was really giving the situation some additional thought. He didn't have the same confident look he had at the beginning of the conversation.

"Now, as much as we enjoy standing here and having this conversation with you, we really have other places we need to be," Recker said. "So unless there's something else that needs to be said, or you wanna try something that you won't live long enough to regret, I'd really appreciate you guys stepping aside."

T stood there staring at him for a few seconds. Eventually, he looked over at his friends and motioned for them to move away.

"All right. I'll let you go this time."

"Oh, thanks," Recker said. "So kind. I was getting worried for a minute."

"You're kind of a cocky guy. Cocky guys sometimes need getting pegged down a notch or two to put them in their place."

"See, the thing about that is, you've gotta be better

than the 'cocky guy' to put him in his place. And I don't see anyone here capable of doing that. But I'm certainly willing to let someone try their luck."

Recker's eyes glanced to the left of T, noticing one of the men slowly putting his hand in the right side of his pants. He knew he was most likely reaching for a gun.

"Hey! Before you pull that thing, you better ask your boss first, because before you're able to use that, T is going to be the first one shot."

T instantly spun his head around to see what his underling was doing.

"Yo, what are you doing, man? Put that away! You don't do nothing until I tell you to. Sit tight!"

The man complied and put his hands in the air.

"Who are you?" T asked. "I know you ain't cops."

"Why aren't we?"

"You don't act like cops. Cops would be here talking about arresting us or asking for backup and shit. That wasn't you. You almost daring us to do something. Taunting us. Cops wouldn't do that. At least not the ones we're used to."

"Just call us concerned citizens."

"Who you here visiting?"

"Again, not your business."

"I can find out, you know."

"I'm sure you can," Recker said. "But in regards to that, if I find out you go in there and hassle people or hurt them in trying to find out who we are, we'll come back. And I guarantee you we won't be in as good a mood as we are right now."

"C'mon, T, let us just drop these jokers right here," one of the other men said.

"Man, you got some real dumb-dumbs working for you. You should go on a hiring spree to find some more talent. Honestly, I don't even know how you're even still around with these idiots working for you."

"They got their talents," T said.

"I'm sure they do."

"So you're not gonna tell me nothin'?"

"Nope."

"All right. Consider this your one get out of jail free card. But don't come back here, all right?"

"Why not?" Recker asked. "What'll happen if I do?"

"Maybe you won't like what happens if you do."

"Now I almost have to just to see what does. Well, I should clarify. What you'll attempt to do. Big distinction in trying and succeeding."

"Oh, we'll succeed."

Recker shook his head. "No, you won't. You'll give it your best effort. But believe me, you and your bozo clowns here aren't ready for what's coming for you if you tangle with us. You might be the toughest people on this block. But there's a world out there that's tougher and badder than you can ever dream of being."

"Guess we'll just have to see, then."

"Guess we will."

T directed his boys to step away from the vehicle, giving Recker and Haley plenty of space as they passed them and got in. Once inside the car, Haley took out his gun, holding it on his lap in case they had a little trouble in exiting. They weren't sure if T was good for his word in letting them out without a problem. It turned out that his word was good. At least this time.

They drove away and exited the parking lot without any further trouble. As they left, both Recker and Haley kept looking in the mirrors to see if anything else was coming their way. They weren't being followed, though. T and his men remained standing in the same spot, just staring at them as they eventually drove out of sight.

"Man, I really thought we might have something there for a while," Haley said.

"Yeah, a few of those guys looked like they wanted to shoot it out."

"You did lay it on pretty thick there."

"Those are the types of guys you gotta talk to that way. If they have any idea that you're afraid of them, they'll walk all over you. You gotta put it in their minds that they're not tougher than you."

"Wonder who those guys really are. And if they're involved in Frank's disappearance."

"Yeah. I wonder about that too. Somebody's gonna have to know who they are."

"Maybe David can find them."

"If not, I'm sure Vincent will have an idea," Recker said.

"You know how you get those feelings from time to time?"

"Yeah?"

"I'm getting one now."

"On what?"

"T and his boys. I got a feeling we haven't seen the last of them."

"I get the feeling you're right," Recker replied. "I don't think we've seen the last of them either. Not by a long shot."

5

―――――

Jones swiveled his chair around as he heard the door open. By the looks on their faces, and the faint detection of a sigh on Recker's end, he got the feeling all was not well. Considering he didn't get any calls or messages to say otherwise, he thought it was a strange reaction. But, he figured it was just frustration that they probably didn't uncover anything at Frank's apartment.

"By the looks of things, I'd say you have nothing new for me?" Jones asked.

"I wouldn't say that," Haley answered. "We might have a name."

"A name? For who?"

"Goes by the name of T," Recker replied.

"T? Is that the letter T? Or is it T-e-e? Or perhaps T-e-a? Maybe he's a fan of Lipton."

Recker grinned. "See? All my jokes have rubbed off on you."

Jones shivered as if he were trying to shake things loose. "There's a sobering thought. So who is this T that we're now talking about?"

Recker then recalled their encounter with the small gang outside the apartment.

"So you didn't find anything inside?" Jones said. "But this gang was waiting for you by your car? How did they know it was yours?"

"I assume we were spotted on the way in," Recker responded.

"And we did find something inside," Haley said. "A missing jewelry box."

Jones raised an eyebrow. "Um. I think it's technically impossible to find something that isn't actually there. I mean, you can't say you found something if you can't actually hold it and touch it and see it."

Haley looked at Recker, while pointing with his thumb back to Jones. "Look at Mr. Semantics over here. Have you been watching some comedy improv shows today?"

"No, just hanging around you guys too long. And who is this other guy you talked about?"

"The neighbor," Recker said. "Jamar."

"And how does he fit in?"

"He doesn't at the moment."

"And who is this T?"

"We don't know. We'll need you to look that up."

"Oh, I'll just add that to my never-ending list."

"Speaking of your list, what have you found out so far?" Recker asked.

Jones swiveled his chair around again to face his computer. "Not much, I'm afraid."

"That wasn't what I was hoping for."

"Me neither, but that's where we are."

"What do you have?"

"Well, phone records have not uncovered anything unusual. He doesn't actually appear to use his phone all that much anyway. At least as far as calling or texting. Very few of either, actually. And no calls on the day he didn't show up for work."

"What about the day before?"

Jones shook his head. "That's a goose egg, as well. No calls. No texts."

"Didn't Jamar say he heard Frank talking loud?" Haley asked. "That would indicate there was somebody there in person."

"He couldn't pin down the exact date, though," Recker replied. He then snapped his fingers. "But he did say that he started watching the Sixers game."

"I'll pull up their schedule." Haley quickly scrolled through his phone. "Looks like they played two days before Frank went missing."

Recker looked at Jones. "You have any phone records for that time? They played at what, seven?"

Haley nodded. "Yeah. Finished after nine."

Jones quickly searched. "No. No activity within that time frame."

"Figures," Recker said. "That means whoever he was talking to had to be in person."

"But why would Jamar hear Frank's voice, but not the person he was talking to?"

"The other guy wasn't heated," Haley said. "He was calm. Talking normal, or barely at all. Only explanation."

"Or Frank had a second phone," Recker said.

"That wouldn't make sense. Why would he?"

Recker shrugged. "Didn't say it made sense. Just said it's another possibility."

Jones had another idea. "Is it possible that this Jamar is lying about it and he didn't really hear anything?"

Recker looked at his friend strangely. "Why would he lie about that?"

Jones threw his hands up. "Who knows? Why do people lie about anything? It suits their purpose somehow. And I'm not saying it's a good idea. Just throwing it out there."

Recker put his hand over his mouth and chin as he thought about it. He couldn't think of any reason why Jamar would lie about that.

"I don't see how that makes sense either."

"Like I said, just throwing it out there," Jones replied.

"Well, we probably shouldn't discount anything at this point either. What else do you have?"

"As I said, not much. He didn't have a lot in the bank. A few thousand dollars. That hasn't been touched in the days leading up to his disappearance, or since then. He doesn't appear to own a passport, so him deciding to leave the country on a whim doesn't seem likely, either."

"Credit cards?" Haley asked.

Jones shook his head. "Also a negative. Had one credit card. He had no balance on it, though. And it hasn't been used in over a month."

"Major bills?"

"Nothing that I can find."

"Social media accounts?"

"He had a couple, and he seemed to use them fairly regularly, though nothing since he disappeared."

"What about before then?" Recker asked. "Anything unusual? Threats? Arguments?"

"No, he seemed to enjoy photography and the outdoors. Wildlife. He commented on pictures he thought were interesting or that he liked. Certainly no arguments or snide comments that I could find."

Recker loudly sighed, appearing to be agitated. "This doesn't make sense. Nothing about this guy seems like he should be a target for someone."

"Maybe we're missing the obvious," Haley said.

"Which is?"

"Maybe he wasn't targeted. Maybe the reason he's

missing is completely random. Some accident somewhere."

"Certainly a possibility," Recker replied. "What about his car? License plate hit anywhere?"

"He did not own one," Jones answered. "Took public transportation everywhere he went. Or walked, I suppose."

"Have you looked up his bus or transit passes?"

"Dead end."

"So you're telling me you have nothing?"

"Well, yes. But that's what I told you in the beginning."

"No, you said, 'not much'. I assumed 'not much' meant something. Even just a small something. Not nothing."

"Are we getting pedantic now?"

Recker shrugged and grinned. "Just striving for accuracy."

"I'll keep that in mind for next time."

"So just to be clear, your 'not much', is nothing, right?"

"For the moment."

"Oh. So can you get on this T, thing, then? I mean, it's not like you have much else going on, it seems."

Jones faked a smile. "I'll move it right up to the top of the list."

"Gee, thanks, Dad."

"Just so I'm clear, and so there are no misunderstandings, there's not much to work with on this T, person."

"Already coming up with excuses as to why you won't get the job done?"

"You're really pushing buttons here, Michael."

Recker let out a laugh, seeing Jones getting hot under the collar.

"Well, you know, I was just..."

Jones put his hand up, not wanting to hear another word. "Out!"

"What?"

Jones pointed toward the door. "Out! If you're just going to stand here and criticize my work, out!"

Recker continued laughing. "OK, OK, I'm done."

Jones gave him a look that suggested he didn't believe him. "Really?"

Recker put his hands up. "Really. I'm done. Since there's nothing to go on..."

"Out!"

"OK, OK, I'm really done now. I promise."

"I mean it. There may be some booby traps in this office that you don't know about, you know."

"Really?"

Now Jones gave the smile. "With all the free time I have here to work on things, you just never know, do you?"

Recker looked over to the wall, where the secret passage was that he didn't know existed for a long period of time. Maybe Jones really had other things worked out. Before the playful banter between the two got out of hand, Haley stepped in.

"So what else do we have going on so far?"

"Not much," Recker answered.

"You don't happen to have anything else to go on with T, do you?" Jones asked. "A picture, perhaps?"

"Well, I was gonna ask for a selfie with my arm around him, but the topic just never seemed to come up."

"I'll take that as a no. Do we even know if he lives in the complex?"

"We do not," Recker replied.

Jones grunted as he typed. "This is not going to be easy."

"Already..."

Jones shot him a look, and Recker immediately discontinued his thought, which was going to be sarcastic.

"Proceed," Recker said.

"What about his daughter?" Haley said. "When's the last time he talked to her?"

"According to my records, it's been a while," Jones answered. "Over a month ago. And just for good measure, I looked into where she's been, and she is out in California. And, I can verify that she was at the Dodgers game in Los Angeles the night before Frank went missing."

"So she's likely out."

"And no mysterious emails or anything?" Recker asked.

"Very infrequent emails that I can find," Jones replied.

"Looks like a hard one, doesn't it?" Haley said.

"That it does."

"Right now, we got two things going for us," Recker said.

"Two?" Haley asked.

"The missing jewelry box."

"That we don't know if there's really anything inside of."

"And T."

"Who won't talk to us without shooting."

"Not great options, there, Michael," Jones said.

"Didn't say they were," Recker replied. "And the jewelry box has to be involved somehow. I mean, why take it if there's nothing inside that's valuable? And two, it would have to be someone close to him that would know about it and what's inside. It would also lead into the theory that whoever was arguing with him that night that Jamar heard about may have taken it."

"And how does T fit? Assuming he's not the one that's taken him or killed him."

"He seems like a guy who always knows what's going on in his neighborhood."

"Even if he does know, I doubt he's the kind who's going to talk to you. Willingly, that is."

"Then we'd just have to make him. Unwillingly."

"Easier said than done," Jones said.

"Most things are."

"And getting him to talk without shooting first is going to be problematic, as well. Not to mention finding out who he is."

Recker shrugged, not concerned with that. "If all else fails, I could just show up and stand in the parking lot again until he shows up."

"I get the feeling you would be lying on the ground dead before you see him again."

"Maybe. But it would be helpful if you found out something about him first. Like a name or an address."

"I'm working on it."

"You know, a guy like T is probably on someone's radar," Haley said. "Someone who already knows what's going down on every block in the city."

"Are you talking about Vincent?" Recker asked.

Haley nodded. "I am. If David punches up a zero, I gotta believe that Vincent's already got this guy in his book."

Recker looked over to the window. "Yeah. I'm sure he does."

"Might be worth a phone call."

Recker glanced at Jones. "Yeah, especially since some people are coming up..."

"I'm warning you, Micheal," Jones said.

Recker chuckled. "In any case, we're already behind the eight ball here. If Vincent can give us something quicker, let's reach out. Frank's been missing for a few days now. Who knows how much time he's got left?"

"If any," Haley said.

Recker pulled out his phone, ready to make the call. "Yeah. We can't afford to wait any longer on this. We need to start making up some time and figure out what's going on here. And we need to do it fast."

6

Recker walked across the grass on his way to the bench that Vincent was sitting on. The crime boss was just staring at the water, watching a few small boats and kayaks go by. Recker gave a half-hearted wave to several of the guards as he passed them. He was a little surprised that he didn't see Malloy around. It was rare that he wasn't near wherever Vincent was.

Recker sat down on the bench. "Thanks for the meet on short notice."

Vincent glanced at him before his eyes quickly returned to the water. "Ah, it's a nice day out, anyway. I wanted to get out and stretch my legs." He then let out a laugh, patting his stomach. "Besides, a little walking outside is good for your health, you know?"

"That's what I hear."

"It seems when you start getting older, everything

you eat ends up straight at the bottom. Doesn't look like you have the same problem, though."

"Well, I move around a lot. Where's Jimmy? Everything OK?"

Vincent waved his hand in the air. "He's attending to another matter. You know, why is it that water has this calming influence? You look at the water, you hear the water, you see people on the water, and it just... it calms your mind. Relaxes you. Why is that?"

"I dunno. I'm sure there have been studies done on it. Some type of reaction to the brain or something."

"Yes, studies. There are studies about everything nowadays. Anyway, enough about that. What's on your mind?"

"I was wondering if you knew anything about a guy named T," Recker said. "Don't have much else on him at the moment. Seems to be in charge of some gang that I don't know the name of. Had a red durag on."

"Where's he operating?"

"Northwest. It's those apartments on..."

Vincent didn't need to hear anything else, though. He already knew who was being talked about. T was someone he'd dealt with before and had his eye on.

"T-Bone."

"You know him?" Recker asked.

"Oh yes. T-Bone Strand. Real name is..." Vincent lowered his head for a moment as he thought. "Darius. Darius Strand."

"Where does the T-Bone come from?"

"I believe because he's tall. And thin."

"Oh. That wasn't what I was expecting."

"So what's your interest in T-Bone?"

"Well, to be honest, I'm not sure I have any."

Vincent looked confused. "Then why are you inquiring about him?"

"I'm looking for someone. In the process of doing that, I ran into T-Bone. Wasn't sure if he might have some connection to what I'm looking at."

"I see. Are you at liberty to tell me what your situation is? Perhaps I can lend some assistance."

"Missing security guard. Works at the same hospital as Mia. Hasn't missed a day in ten years. All of a sudden, doesn't show up. Everyone's concerned, police look into it, nothing to be found. And he hasn't turned up anywhere that we can tell. Hospitals, morgues, nothing. Daughter in California, no other family around that we know of, just seems to have vanished."

"History of mental illness, maybe? Just wandered off somewhere?"

Recker shook his head. "No history of it."

"That's a tough one for sure."

"So we went to his apartment, looked around, talked to a neighbor, figured out there's a missing jewelry box, and nothing else. Went back to our car and found T-Bone waiting for us, asking what we were doing, had some words with him, and now I'm just wondering if he might be involved somehow."

"My initial reaction would be doubtful."

"Why?"

"Doesn't sound like T-Bone's style," Vincent said. "He and his group... they're not the most... delicate, shall we say? They're not exactly the type who make elderly people go missing without anyone knowing about it. Don't get me wrong. They'll make people go missing. Permanently. But they're not exactly shy or deceitful about it."

"So you don't think they'd kidnap him for some reason?"

"Not unless he stole some of their merchandise and they're looking for it."

"Drugs?"

Vincent nodded. "Among other things. But that's their main play."

"Hard to believe he'd be mixed up in that."

"That's why I don't think they'd be involved in his disappearance. If they were, you'd likely have found your victim by now. Probably lying on the sidewalk with some holes in him."

"Seems like a dangerous group."

Vincent shrugged. "Can be if you don't know how to handle them."

"Kind of surprising that you're letting them walk around without a leash on."

"They're small-time right now. I've had conversations with T-Bone. He knows where he stands. If he gets out of line, or gets too big for his britches, he knows he'll receive a visit. As of now, he mostly operates out of a small area. I'm OK with that. As long as he has no aspirations of expanding, steps on my toes, or infringes on my business, he's OK. But make no mistake, I've got my eyes on him. I'm watching. And he's not the only one, believe me. There's others like him around. But they all know their place."

"So you're doubtful he's involved?"

"I am. Unless there's something you don't know yet, such as this guy working with them in some capacity. But if the guy's clean, it would be surprising to me if T-Bone's the guy you're looking for."

"Do you think it's possible you could set up a meeting with him for me?"

"For what purpose?" Vincent asked.

"Seemed like he's a big man around there. Maybe he has an idea of what's going on. If he's got eyes and ears stashed there, maybe someone knows something. Based on our last encounter, I'd be wary of just showing up uninvited."

"Probably a wise move. I'll see what I can do. Any preferences on time and place?"

Recker shook his head. "Doesn't matter to me. Anywhere. And as soon as possible."

"I'll get to work on it. I'll let you know when I get something."

"I appreciate it."

Vincent nudged Recker on the arm. "You know,

you'll probably find out this guy you're looking for has got a double life or something."

"What makes you think that?"

"Just a guess. When people go missing, you usually find some skeleton in their closet. Some secret they didn't want to get out. And then, bam, it bursts out at the wrong time. It finally surfaces. It's probably no different with this guy."

"Yeah. Maybe."

"We've all got those things we think we put in the rearview mirror. They're out of sight for a while, then it just bubbles up to the top. Five will get you ten that that's what you're dealing with here. Some skeleton in the closet. I'll bank on it."

Considering what they had to work with so far, Recker really wasn't in any position to argue. It certainly could play out just as Vincent was describing. Or maybe he had T-Bone pinned wrong. Maybe that was unlikely. Vincent rarely, if ever, had anyone pinned wrong. He always knew who he was dealing with. Sometimes more than they knew themselves. In his line of work, Vincent couldn't afford to be sloppy. If he thought T-Bone wasn't good for it, he probably wasn't. Still, until he had more facts to go on, Recker couldn't rule anything out yet.

With nothing else needing to be said, Recker and Vincent shook hands and went their separate ways. Recker got up and walked away, heading back to his car. As he walked, his text ringer sounded. He quickly took out his phone and checked it. It was from Haley.

"Hey. Call me as soon as you get this. We got a problem."

Once Recker reached his car, he leaned up against the driver's side door as he called his partner. Haley picked up on the second ring.

"So what's this problem?" Recker asked.

"Looks like we got a body."

Recker sighed and looked down. It was what he was fearing would happen sooner or later.

"Where'd they find it?"

"It's not Frank's," Haley answered.

"What? Then whose body is it and how does it pertain to us?"

"It's Jamar's."

"What?!"

"Apparently it was found this morning."

"We just talked to him yesterday," Recker said.

"I know. And today he's dead."

"Are you sure?"

"David got the alert. Police responded to his address three hours ago after a report of a gunshot. Dead on arrival."

Recker loudly sighed again, clearly unhappy, as he put his hand on the back of his neck and looked down at the ground.

"How does this make sense?"

"It doesn't," Haley replied. "Not yet."

"So we're looking for Frank, who we can't find. Then we talk to his neighbor, who just so happens to get killed the day after we talk to him."

"Kinda makes you wonder."

"Yeah. It does. Like, did someone know we talked to him, and they were afraid of what else he might tell us?"

"Who around there does that sound like? Watching. Waiting."

"T-Bone."

"Who?"

"Oh, yeah, Vincent told me his name. T-Bone. Or Darius Strand."

"Maybe Mr. Strand might know a little something," Haley said.

"Vincent thinks otherwise. Well, at least as far as Frank's disappearance."

"I don't know. I think we might need another round with him."

"I agree. Vincent's gonna set something up for us. At least there won't be any shooting that way. Maybe we'll get some answers."

"Be nice if we could get some. Or even one."

"Give David T's name. See if he can start running stuff down."

"Will do. You heading back to the office?"

"Unless something else comes up," Recker answered. "But I think having a discussion with T-

Bone is our next move. Until then, I think we're just swimming around in circles."

"Or we could look into Jamar's background. See if something comes up that's fishy."

"Any preliminary word on what happened to him?"

"Looks like self-inflicted."

Recker huffed. "Self-inflicted, my ass. You mean, made to look like he killed himself."

"I don't get it. I don't understand why this guy was killed. It didn't seem like he knew anything more than what he told us. Unless he was holding back."

"Remember, it's not always what you know. It's what other people *think* you might know. There's a difference. Somebody might've thought he knew a whole lot more. And maybe he did know more, and he didn't even know it himself yet."

"Like he saw something and didn't know what it was when he saw it?"

"Something like that."

"Guess we're not gonna know now."

"Maybe," Recker said. "But it seems like things are starting to spiral quickly here. Let's get to the bottom of things before we find another body."

"There's still one looming."

"I know. But let's see if we can change that."

"That's gonna be a tall order."

"Yeah, but let's try to fill it. Somebody has to."

7

Recker walked in the door, almost immediately getting greeted with a kiss from his girlfriend.

"You're just in time. Dinner's just about ready."

"Smells good," Recker said.

"Can you guess what it is?"

Recker lifted his nose and sniffed. "Let's see. Chicken?"

Mia smiled. "Yep."

"Mashed potatoes."

"Right."

"Corn?"

"You got it."

"Gravy?"

"You don't really smell all that, do you?"

Recker laughed. "Not really. I do smell the chicken. And you know I like mashed potatoes with it. And I like gravy on top of it. And I like corn on the side. Just putting two and two together."

They kissed again, then walked into the kitchen.

"Are you hungry?"

"I can definitely eat," Recker replied.

They sat down at the table, and took a few bites of their food. Mia had the case on her mind, though.

"Any leads on Frank yet?"

Recker could only shake his head. "Not really, no."

"Where could he be?"

"I don't know."

As Recker continued to eat, Mia stared at his face for a minute. She was studying it, trying to figure out what it meant. He definitely had a way of holding things in when he didn't want to say something. But his face said differently. By now, she knew the little quirks his face made. A little twitch of his cheek, or a prolonged frown, a slight raise of an eyebrow, they all said something to Mia. This was no different.

"What is it?"

Recker seemed startled by the question. "Hmm?"

"What are you trying not to tell me?"

"Nothing."

"Something happened, didn't it? Something's wrong? I can tell. You have that face that says something's wrong."

Recker chuckled. "No I don't."

"You do. You've got that 'I know something that I'm not going to tell her face'."

"I didn't realize I had that face."

"You do. You found him already, didn't you? And you don't want to tell me?"

"No, we didn't find him. I promise. We haven't found him."

"And you don't know what happened?"

"Not yet, no."

"Then what else is there?" Mia asked. "And don't tell me nothing. I can tell there is. Just come out with it. I can handle it."

"It's... not about Frank. Well, it kind of is, but not specifically him."

"What?"

"We talked to Frank's neighbor yesterday. His name was Jamar. We looked in Frank's apartment, and Jamar told us there was a jewelry box missing. That's all we've got on that front."

Mia pointed at his head. "Then what's with that face now?"

Recker took a deep breath. "Because we found out earlier that Jamar is now dead."

"What? How?"

"Police think it's suicide. Gunshot to the side of the head."

"You don't believe that, do you? That's a really big coincidence."

"You know I don't believe in coincidences," Recker said. "The day after we talk to him? Nah. Somebody knew we were there and wanted to shut him up. They were either afraid of what he told us or afraid of what he *might* tell us."

"I don't get it. What's going on?"

Recker could only shake his head. "I wish I knew. But I don't. Not yet."

"And you don't have an inkling?"

"I really don't. As far as we can tell, there's nothing in Frank's background that would make him a target. He wasn't in debt. He had no criminal history. He didn't hang around bad people that we can see. So where is he?" Recker threw his hands up. "I don't know."

"What about his daughter?"

"Hasn't spoken to her in over a month. And she was at a Dodgers game when he disappeared."

"Don't you think that's weird? Not speaking to your only daughter in that long of a time?"

"They apparently weren't close. It happens. Kids drift away. Have their own lives. Parents fade to the background."

"I guess."

"You haven't heard any other rumors at the hospital, have you?" Recker asked.

"About where Frank is? No. Everyone's still kind of in shock that he isn't there. Still can't believe it."

They talked a little while longer, though they didn't get anywhere or uncover any new information. They just kept rehashing the same things. Finally, Recker's phone rang to interrupt the conversation. He answered.

"Wasn't expecting a call so soon."

"Well, this situation seems like it's got you tied up in knots," Vincent said. "I figured I'd do what I could to get you in the ballgame."

"I appreciate that."

"Anyway, T-Bone will meet with you in two hours. If that's agreeable with you?"

Recker looked at his watch. "Yeah, I can make it."

"Great. I'll finalize it on his end."

"Where at?"

"In front of the complex. He'll be waiting for you."

"Does he know about me?" Recker asked.

"I told him you were an associate of mine and to cooperate with you. He shouldn't give you any problems."

"I hope not."

"But, just as an added precaution, I'll have Jimmy meet you there. Just to break bread, so to speak."

"Thanks."

"Don't mention it. I hope he can give you what you're looking for. Or at least some answers."

"I do too."

Recker put his phone down and looked at his girl-friend. She already knew what the deal was.

"So you're leaving, huh?"

Recker gave her a sheepish smile. "Maybe this guy

knows something about Frank. Or what happened to Jamar. We need a lead. And right now we don't have any."

"I understand. You won't be gone all night, will you?"

"I wouldn't think so. But I don't know what he might tell me either."

"I get it. And I want to know what happened with Frank. You have to go. Taking Chris with you?"

Recker nodded. "He's like American Express. I don't leave home without him."

"Just be careful."

"Always am."

Mia then gave him a seductive look. "So maybe if you're not done too late, we can have some alone time later?"

Recker smiled. "Well if that's the case, I'll make sure I'm not done too late."

They kissed, then Recker picked up his phone again to call his partner. After a few rings, Haley answered.

"Silencer Security Services, what's your emergency?"

Recker laughed. "Funny. How long have you been working on that one?"

"Oh, just had it in my back pocket for a few days now."

"Nice. Anyway, put your soup to the side for a little bit."

"How'd you know I was eating soup?"

"Wait, are you?"

"Yeah. Bacon and potato."

"Really?"

"Yeah. You got me on camera or something?"

"No. Maybe I'm just psychic or something."

"Scary," Haley said. "Anyway, what's on the agenda?"

"Vincent's got us a meeting with T-Bone. Two hours from now."

"Nice. I can eat my soup and still be ready. Are we sure we're getting a ceasefire? I don't wanna go in there and find out we're target practice, you know?"

"I hear you. But no, Vincent said Malloy's gonna meet us there to make sure nothing goes down."

"Oh. Good. I won't bring my fifteen shotguns with us, then."

"Hey, I'm not sure I'd go that far," Recker said. "Make sure you're armed. Hopefully we won't need it, though."

"I'll just be happy if we actually get something useful out of this."

"So will I. I'll swing down in about half an hour and pick you up."

"Sounds good. I'll be ready. Let's hope this trip won't be a waste."

"I got one of those feelings," Recker said. "Something tells me it won't be. I'm not sure why. I just got a feeling we'll get something out of this."

"Hopefully it won't be lead."

Recker laughed. "Yeah, that would be unfortunate, wouldn't it? But no, I think we're gonna get something we can really use here. Whatever that is. I don't know what, but something."

8

Recker pulled into the parking lot of the apartment complex, not immediately seeing anyone he recognized. There were a few people walking around, though they didn't appear to be aimlessly wandering. Once he found a spot, he and Haley sat there for a few minutes, checking out their surroundings.

"Where'd they say the meeting was happening?" Haley asked.

"Said right out front."

"I don't see anyone."

Recker checked the time. "We still got five minutes. Malloy should be here too. He's usually not late for things."

They saw a few cars go by as they waited. Finally, they saw a vehicle pull up to the front of the building. It was Malloy. He got out of the car and waited.

"Should we join him?" Haley asked.

"No, not yet."

"Why not?"

"Not until T-Bone's there too."

"Afraid of a drive-by?"

"I'll admit it did cross my mind," Recker replied. "We don't really know this guy. And even though Vincent seems to be all right with him, who's to say he doesn't have bigger and grander plans? Wouldn't get much bigger than getting us and Malloy in the same spot and knocking us all off."

"Good point."

"So, let's just pump the brakes until he shows up."

"I doubt Vincent would let Malloy show up for that if there was any inkling of it, though."

"I agree. It's probably not likely. But still. Better safe than sorry."

Barely another minute went by until they noticed a group of men walking along the buildings, going towards Malloy's position.

"Doesn't that look like our guys?"

Recker stared at the group for a few seconds. "That's them. T-Bone out in front."

They still waited in their car for a minute to make sure everything was on the up-and-up. Then, once they felt good about the situation, they got out of their car and approached the building as well.

"Yo, we're meeting with these guys again?" one of

the men said, noticing Recker and Haley come towards them.

"Just be quiet," T-Bone replied. "I got this."

Once Recker and Haley got there, they shook hands with Malloy.

"Thanks for coming," Recker said.

Malloy grinned. "Well, it's not like I had much choice in the matter."

"True."

"You had some pretty big talk the last time you were here," T-Bone said.

"So did you," Recker replied.

"Yeah. I ain't forget it either."

"Can we just stop with the tough-talk nonsense and get down to business?"

"I don't see what business I got with you. I'm only here cause Vincent asked me to meet with you. That's it. I ain't here cause I want to."

"I don't really care why you're here. As long as you are. But I told Vincent I was only meeting with you. And you alone."

"Not without my crew here."

"Listen, we can do this the easy way or the hard way," Recker said. "But one way or another, I'm gonna get what I want."

"There's that tough talk again."

Sensing that things were beginning to get out of hand, Malloy stepped in.

"Hey, hey, listen. We're not here to see who's got the

bigger stones or anything. We're here for a meeting. Let's act accordingly."

"Tell your guys to take a hike," Recker said.

T-Bone shook his head. "They ain't going nowhere."

Malloy tapped T-Bone on the arm. "Get them out of here. This meeting will go on as advertised under the conditions specified. Unless you'd like me to inform Vincent that you were uncooperative?"

A solemn face came over T-Bone. He was tough. He liked to do things his own way. But he had no interest in getting into a war with Vincent. That was one he knew he wouldn't win. He didn't have the manpower. Or the ambition, really. He was content with how things were for him. He turned to face his guys.

"All right, you guys take off. I'll catch up with you all later."

"You sure about this?" one of them asked.

T-Bone turned his head toward Recker.

Recker put his arms out to his side in a non-threatening manner. "All I want is some information. I'm not here for anything else. And I don't care what you're doing as long as it doesn't interfere with me. Once I get what I want, you don't have to see me anymore."

T-Bone motioned for his guys to take off. His men were still hesitant, but they eventually complied.

"What makes you think I have any information for you? I ain't no snitch."

Recker grinned. "Well, I guess that's what we'll have to talk about."

"Probably shouldn't do this out here," Malloy said.

"You got someplace to go?"

T-Bone smiled. "What do I look like? The maintenance man? Think I got keys to just go in whatever place I want?"

"Let's just use my car," Malloy said. "I'll pull around back."

Everyone piled into Malloy's car, with Haley getting in the front passenger seat, while Recker and T-Bone got into the back. Once they were inside, Malloy started the car and pulled it around to the back of the buildings. There were fewer cars back there, and though there were a few basketball courts, nobody was playing at the present time.

"So what's all this about?" T-Bone asked.

"Looking for information about a guy named Frank," Recker answered. "Lived in B9. He's missing."

"So? What's that got to do with me?"

"Well, that's what we were here for yesterday when you greeted us. Thought maybe you were keeping an eye on us."

"Yeah, I was keeping an eye on you, but not for that. I just wanted to make sure you weren't some outsider trying to sneak in on my territory."

"Well you can put that to rest. I don't care about your territory."

"I don't know what happened to Frank, man. Can't help you with that one."

"So you knew him?"

"Man, I know everyone that lives here."

"What about Jamar?" Haley asked. "Frank's neighbor?"

"What about him?"

"He just happens to turn up dead after we talk to him? I assume you had nothing to do with that either?"

"You would be very correct," T-Bone replied.

"So what you're saying is... that you're incompetent," Recker said.

"Say what now?"

"You're supposed to be in charge here. You act like some big tough leader. And yet you have people disappearing and getting killed right under your nose and you don't know a thing about it? So which is it? You know something about this stuff or you really have no clue about your operation?"

"You're trying to get a rise out of me."

"No, I'm just trying to get you to tell the truth. There are people worried about Frank. They wanna know what happened to him. And now his neighbor's dead too. A lot of things that don't add up here. Maybe you can help unravel it."

"Look, I really don't know what happened with Jamar. Word I got was he shot himself. Suicide."

"Yeah, that's the word," Recker said. "But it's not. He

didn't kill himself. Someone did it for him. The question is why?"

T-Bone shook his head. "I can't help you with that question. I don't know. I wasn't even around here when it happened. I was doing business elsewhere, when I got over here, there were a bunch of police here swarming around. And the word I got was it was suicide. I took it at face value. So I can't help you with that."

"And Frank? C'mon, man. He's a guy in his sixties not bothering anybody. Did you have a beef with him?"

"Frank? Hell no, man. He was an all right dude."

"Jamar said Frank had it out with some of the local gangs," Haley said. "Probably meaning you too?"

"Nah, it wasn't like that. It was nothing personal."

"Then what was it?"

"If Frank was hanging around or walking outside and he saw something, he'd always speak up. Especially if it was a younger kid, teenager, guy in his early twenties, things like that. He felt he had to look out for people. Try and make sure they didn't go down the wrong hole, you know?"

"And you didn't have a problem with that?"

"No. How can you fault a guy for looking out for the younger kids?"

"Even if that runs counter to your business?"

"It's not like that. He didn't try to meddle into things. He just tried to give people guidance. That's it. You've gotta respect someone like that. Someone from the outside wouldn't understand. There was no beef. Even if Frank interrupted a deal with a high school kid or something, we just moved on. There's no bad blood. You respect the fact that Frank's watching out for these kids, but it's not like we lost business or nothing. We just moved on to the next customer. There was no hostility or cursing or anything. That's just how it is, man."

"OK, even if we believe that, something had to happen to him," Recker said. "He didn't just decide to leave his apartment and not come back one day. Something happened."

T-Bone made a face and sighed, looking like someone who had more on his mind. It wasn't lost on Recker.

"C'mon, you can tell us," Recker said. "Whatever it is, it won't leave this car. If it's something with your crew or someone else, nobody else needs to know. I'm not trying to get anyone else jammed up over anything. I just wanna know what's going on and find him. That's it."

T-Bone rubbed his face. "All right, look, a few days back, I don't know exactly what day it was or anything. It was a few days before Frank went missing is all I know. I saw him in an argument with some dude."

"Where?"

T-Bone pointed to the basketball courts. "Right out here. They were just walking and talking. But it was getting heated. I could tell that."

"How could you tell?"

"I was a good distance away, but I could hear their voices being raised. I couldn't hear what they were saying, but they were both motioning and moving their bodies around, you know, the way people do when they get mad. And both their faces were getting red. It was definitely heated, no doubt."

"Who was this guy? You know him?"

"Nah, never seen him before. He's not from around here, I know that."

"So he didn't live here?" Recker asked.

"No way."

"What did this guy look like?"

"Uh, younger guy, I guess. In his thirties, probably. Short hair, no facial hair, some tattoos on his arms. Average height and weight, I guess. Wasn't too much about him, really. Pretty average-looking dude."

"Recognize any of the tattoos or anything? Specific gang or something?"

"Nah, couldn't really see anything specific. I could just see that he had some."

"And you never saw this guy before?"

T-Bone shook his head. "Never. Never seen him since either."

"How long did this argument last?"

"Couldn't say. I watched them for a minute, then I had to go. Business was calling."

"Did you ever go inside Frank's apartment?" Recker asked.

"Nah, we weren't that close."

"But Jamar was?"

T-Bone shrugged. "I guess. I never asked them."

"Anything else you can add?"

"Yeah. This never came from me."

"You really didn't give us much," Haley said.

"Never said I had much."

"There's nothing else you can tell us?" Recker asked.

"Not that I can think of. All I know is I saw him arguing with this dude. That's it. That's all I can tell you. Find this dude, and he'll probably know more than I do."

"All right. I guess that's it."

"Great. Now can I get back to my crew now?"

Recker rolled his window down. It was just in time to hear the sounds of gunfire. Multiple rounds were being followed.

"Where's that coming from?" Haley asked.

Recker pointed to the north. "Sounds like that way."

"Hey, let's go over and check it out," T-Bone said.

"Why?"

"C'mon, c'mon. I've just been here answering your questions. Let's just go and see."

Recker gave Malloy a nod, who immediately started driving. He looked over at T-Bone, who had a worried look on his face.

"I got a bad feeling about this, man. A real bad feeling."

Recker didn't have the same feeling this time. He was sure something was happening. What that was, he didn't know. He was willing to go along here, but he didn't think this would concern them much. Unless it somehow had to do with Frank, which seemed unlikely.

As they got closer, the gunfire suddenly stopped. It was now quiet again. Malloy kept driving, only taking a few more minutes to reach their destination of where they thought the gunfire was happening.

Malloy stopped the car, and each of the men stared at the scene. None of them got out initially. They were all stunned. This wasn't something any of them were expecting. Especially T-Bone. His friends and crew were dead. Lying out there, shot full of holes.

Recker wasn't sure how this pertained to them, but now it felt like it did. Somehow. It couldn't have been a coincidence. T-Bone's crew ends up dead the moment he shows up to talk to the leader. Just like with Jamar. Something was going on here. He didn't have a clue as to what it could be. But something was going on.

9

Upon seeing his friends lying there, T-Bone jumped out of the car and ran over to them. Recker, Haley, and Malloy got out of the car also, and casually strolled over to them. They could see that T-Bone was genuinely upset at the fate of his friends, and had tears coming out of his eyes.

T-Bone looked back at them for a moment. "I'm gonna find out who did this! I promise you that! I'm gonna find out who did this!"

Recker stared at him, thinking this could help them. He didn't have much sympathy for the dead, however. He didn't know them, and as far as he was concerned, they probably had what was coming to them for selling drugs to teenage children. But even though he didn't feel badly about what happened, the loss of anyone's life was never something to be celebrated. He wasn't going to jump up and down over their deaths. He just wasn't going to feel sad about it either.

"This could've been me," T-Bone said, holding one of his friends in his arms. "I could've been with them."

"Be thankful that you're not," Malloy replied.

T-Bone got up and marched over to the other three. "You think this got something to do with what you're looking into?"

Recker briefly glanced at the dead bodies. "Tough to say."

As Recker thought about it in his mind, he couldn't think of a reason why it would be connected. It sure felt like it was. A lot of dead bodies were dropping all of a sudden. But why that was? He couldn't say.

"Why would a missing hospital security guard and his dead neighbor have anything to do with your friends getting killed?" Recker asked.

"I don't know. But I aim to find out. Maybe because I'm standing here talking to you."

"But how would anyone...?"

Recker stopped mid-sentence as he turned his head around, looking in different directions.

"You got something?" Haley asked.

Recker didn't answer at first, as he continued spinning his head around. Something was eating at him. Nothing made sense except for one thing. They were being watched. They had to be. It was the only explanation.

Haley and Malloy started looking around, as well, thinking their friend was on to something he hadn't shared yet. Recker completely turned his body around until he got back to his original position.

"Somebody's watching," Recker said.

The others got a concerned look on their faces as they continued looking around. Nobody saw anything alarming, though.

"What do you mean, somebody's watching?" Haley asked. "Who? And where?"

"I don't know. But they're out there."

"How do you know?" Malloy asked.

"I don't know it. I feel it."

"Who'd be watching us?" T-Bone asked.

"Same people that killed your friends here. And probably killed Jamar. And probably know what happened with Frank."

"Who are these people?"

Recker could only shrug. "Guess that's what we need to find out."

"Man, there ain't nobody out there watching."

Suddenly, they heard the screeching of car tires. It was close by. A vehicle raced in front from behind them. Recker and company quickly turned around and saw the car speeding towards them. Their lights weren't on to try to hide their movements, though the racing of the engine gave it away.

"Hit the dirt!" Recker said.

The popping sounds of automatic rifles filled the

air. Recker and team flopped onto the ground or hugged the car as close as they could to shield themselves from the bullets that were incoming.

As the car raced away, they got out their guns and were about to return fire, though by this point, it was too late. But they'd soon get another chance. Instead of flying out of the parking lot, the car turned around, ready to make another pass at them.

All four men fired at the car as it passed by, as their own car got littered with bullet holes. Seconds later, the car was gone.

"Anybody get a make or model?" Haley asked, getting to his knees.

Recker stood up, putting his gun in his holster, looking in the direction the car just left. "Nah, something dark."

"Damn," Malloy huffed, looking at his car. "Shot to pieces."

The others looked at his vehicle.

"Tires are still up," Recker said. "Does it run?"

"I'll find out," Malloy answered, getting behind the wheel. The car started right up.

"That's something, at least."

"Vincent's not gonna like this."

"At least it's only the car that's shot up."

"That's true."

"How'd you know they were out there?" Haley asked.

Recker continued looking around, not sure they were out of danger yet. "Like I said, I didn't know it. Just felt it."

"How? What tipped you off?"

"It was something T-Bone said. Maybe his friends were killed because we were here."

"What sense does that make? How would they know?"

"Exactly," Recker said. "How would they know? Unless they were watching. Think about it. How would they know we talked to Jamar yesterday?"

"They had eyes on you," Malloy answered.

"That's gotta be it. What else makes sense?"

"Who'd be watching this place?"

Recker turned toward T-Bone. "You seem to know this place better than anyone. Who'd be watching?"

"Man, I don't know. Nobody's watching. Or should be watching."

"No competition lately? Bad blood with anyone? Rumors about a new gang looking to come in and take over? Anything like that?"

T-Bone shook his head. "No. Not that I've heard, anyway. Everything's been going smooth. At least till you guys showed up."

"Frank disappeared before we showed up."

"So whoever these people are, they were watching us when we talked to Jamar," Haley said. "And they were watching tonight when we showed up again to talk to T-Bone. Why take out his crew? I mean, we figured maybe Jamar knew something, but T-Bone says they don't know anything."

All Recker could do was shrug. He didn't have any answers. Only more questions. He didn't know why someone would be watching. Only that somebody was. That seemed obvious now.

"Why not go for us first?" T-Bone asked.

"Your friends walking around were probably easier targets," Recker replied.

"This don't make no sense, man."

"You can say that again."

"I mean, we got nothing to do with Frank. Or Jamar. Why target us?"

Recker didn't have a response. He had no idea. About anything. It was all still a mystery. They didn't have time to continue discussing the matter, though. They heard police sirens in the background.

"That's probably for us," Haley said.

"Looks like I gotta go," T-Bone replied.

"I'll catch up with you later," Malloy told the others.

Recker and Haley immediately turned around and started jogging back to their car. T-Bone walked in the opposite direction. Malloy was able to drive his car quickly out of the lot before the patrol cars showed up.

Once they got back to their car, Recker and Haley jumped in, then quickly drove off. The sirens were getting closer, but they were coming from the other end of the complex. They'd be able to sneak out the front. Now out on the road, the pair continued discussing their problem.

"What the hell is going on here, Mike?"

Recker puffed. "I don't know. I really don't know."

"Like T-Bone said, this doesn't make a lick of sense."

"I know it."

"And where is Frank? If all these other bodies are turning up, why isn't his?"

Recker couldn't answer. He just didn't know. Haley had other theories that he threw out there.

"Hey, I got a crazy idea. I mean, this is really out there."

"Might as well say it," Recker said. "Can't be any crazier than what's actually probably happening."

Haley chuckled to himself, realizing how far out there this would sound. "I don't even know if I can say it."

"Just throw it out there."

"What if Frank is actually the one behind all this?"

He glanced over at his partner, anticipating a look to suggest he was crazy. He wasn't disappointed. Recker gave him the look he was expecting.

"I know. I know. It's crazy."

"Maybe it's not as crazy as we think," Recker said.

"I mean, think about it. He's gone, his neighbor's

dead, and all these other guys are dead. His jewelry box is missing. Maybe he's the one that took it."

"And he's just hanging around, going all scorched earth on everybody?"

Haley threw his hands up. "Who knows? Maybe the guy just snapped."

"People who snap don't usually calculate like this. They don't snap and then take a few days to kill their neighbor. They usually just do it right away."

"There are always exceptions."

"And he just mows down the local gang?"

"Fed up with their nonsense."

"You don't really believe this, do you?" Recker asked.

"Uh, no? I mean, I don't think so. But like I said, just throwing it out there. I know how it sounds. That's why I said it was crazy."

Recker sighed. "As crazy as it does sound, it's probably not something we can completely dismiss yet. Not until we have something better and more concrete to go on. I just have a hard time believing that this guy would go off the crazy train like this."

"I'm struggling to come up with another reason. What's the connection between all of them if it isn't him that's pulling the trigger here?"

Recker couldn't think of anything. "I don't know. There must be a reason somewhere. At some point, hopefully we'll find it."

"Maybe it'll find us."

"That would work too. I wouldn't mind if things just dropped into our lap."

"Not sure we can count on that," Haley said.

"I'm not counting on it. Just hoping. Hoping and praying."

10

———

Recker and Haley arrived at the office at the same time, with Recker having a bag of bagels in hand. He put them down on the counter as the others came over. He glanced at Jones, who was giving him a look.

"What?" Recker asked.

"You have nothing else to say?"

Recker looked at his other partner, thinking that maybe he missed something. Haley just gave him a shrug, not knowing what Jones had on his mind. Jones put his arms out, as if he were already tired of waiting for a response.

"Nothing?"

Recker laughed. "I don't know what you want me to say. What are we talking about?"

Jones rolled his eyes and looked up at the ceiling,

stretching his arms out again. "He doesn't know what I'm talking about, he says."

Recker turned his head around. "Am I living in an alternate universe right now or something? Because I really don't know what's going on here."

Jones sighed. "The incident last night?"

"Oh. Yeah? What about it?"

"So nonchalant. Like it's nothing. Like it happens every day."

"I'm sorry, Dad. I told you about it last night."

"You sent me a text summarizing the events," Jones replied. "A little more details would have been nice. You made it sound like, 'oh, shot at, no biggie, tomorrow's another day. Move on'. I mean, do these events not even bother you anymore."

"Well of course it bothers me. But it was already late. And, uh, well, Mia was waiting for me. And I figured we'd talk about it today anyway."

Jones let out another sigh and rubbed his forehead. "Could you explain, in a little bit greater detail, exactly what happened?"

"Well, sure, Dad."

Jones gritted his teeth, hating when his partner called him that. Recker then recalled the previous night's events.

"Think you can pull up any security footage from the area?" Recker asked.

"All you told me is that it's a dark-colored car."

"Maybe we'll find one with a bullet hole in it."

"You hit it?" Jones asked.

"I'd imagine that one of us did. There were four of us shooting at it. I gotta believe that one of us got it."

"Plus it was at night," Haley said. "Not as much traffic."

"Also darker and tougher to see," Jones replied. "And it was the late evening. Not two in the morning. There is still some traffic at that time of night."

"So you're already giving excuses as to why you won't find it?" Recker asked.

"Michael."

Recker grinned. "OK, OK."

"I will do my best with the limited amount of information I have to work with."

"That's all I can ask, Doctor."

Jones shook his head, took his bagel, and went back to his seat. Recker smiled, then put some cream cheese on his bagel. Before he had a chance to take a bite, though, his phone rang. It was a familiar number. He wasn't anticipating Vincent calling, but considering the events of the previous night, he thought it was understandable if he wanted to get things clear in his own mind, even though Recker was sure that Malloy told him all about it.

"Sorry about your car," Recker said.

Vincent laughed. "That's the way it goes, right? Better to have holes in the vehicles than holes in the people."

"Can say that again. I'm not sure what else I can

add, though. Didn't Malloy tell you about what happened?"

"He did. And he was very thorough, as usual. But that's not what I'm calling about today."

"Oh. Something else come up?"

Vincent chuckled. "Interesting metaphor you use there. In a manner of speaking, yes, something else has come up. Very literally."

"What do you mean?"

"I mean a body. One has literally popped up out of the river. It's surfaced."

Recker was starting to get an uneasy feeling in the pit of his stomach. "And how does that concern me?"

"You're looking for a missing person, are you not? I thought that might be him."

"You're not sure who it is?"

"Not at the moment. It's at the Medical Examiner's Office on North Broad Street. Just came in this morning. They've gotta go through the usual tests and whatnot. Who knows how long that'll take? And I don't know in what condition the body is in. So, I'm just passing all the information along to you if you want to take it further."

"Thanks. I'll have to see if David can monitor it somehow."

"No need," Vincent said. "I have some contacts down there."

"Of course you do."

"There's a woman who works there named Cheryl.

She'll be waiting for you. I told her you'd be there in about an hour. I hope that works for you. She's busy. She has other things to do, you know?"

"No, that works," Recker responded. "We can make it."

"Good. I'm not sure if I'm rooting for you to find what you're looking for or not in this instance. Whatever the case, I hope you find some answers. One way or another."

"Thanks. I appreciate it."

Once Recker hung up, both his partners immediately had questions, overhearing his conversation.

"So what can we make?" Haley asked.

"And what am I monitoring?" Jones said.

"Perky ears this morning, huh?" Recker replied.

"Should I get my pen out so I can add it to my list?"

"No, I think this will only concern Chris and I for now."

"Oh. I feel left out."

"So where are we headed?" Haley asked.

"Medical Examiner's Office."

"Why? Who died?"

"Don't know yet," Recker answered. "Vincent said a body came in this morning after getting pulled from the river."

"Well, who's he think it might be?"

"We're looking for a missing person, aren't we?"

"He thinks it's Frank?"

Recker shrugged. "He's not sure. He just wanted to pass the information along."

"And how are you going to tell whether it's him or not?" Jones asked. "Are you going to just show up and... wait, no, I got it. Vincent has a contact down there who's going to show you in, doesn't he?"

Recker smiled. "You know him too well."

"Of course he does. Because... why wouldn't he? He has a contact everywhere."

"Well, he is Vincent. He wouldn't have lasted this long if he wasn't well connected."

"So when are we making this meeting?" Haley asked.

Recker looked at his watch. "One hour."

"We better get moving, then. Traffic and all."

"Yeah. Guess we're taking our bagels on the run."

"I'll start working on our friends from last night," Jones said. "See if I can pull something out of the air."

"All right, let us know."

Recker and Haley got themselves ready, then left the office. It took them about forty-five minutes to reach their destination. The entrance was on Callowhill Street, so they parked a little further up the road, then walked to the building. Just as they reached it, a woman stepped outside.

"You don't happen to be Cheryl, are you?" Recker asked.

She looked the two of them over. "You the guys Vincent sent?"

"We are."

"Right on time. Punctual. I like it. I was just coming outside to wait for you. Follow me."

As they followed the woman inside, they conversed with a little small talk for a bit. After a few minutes, they turned their attention to business.

"Either of you squeamish or anything?"

"Uh, no," Recker answered. "Is it that bad?"

"No, but the sight of a dead body sometimes has a way of doing funny things to people who otherwise consider themselves to have a strong stomach."

"Oh. No, we're good."

"Great. So how do you know Vincent?"

"How do you know Vincent?" Recker asked.

Cheryl brushed the question off, and went back to the topic at hand. "Anyway, this body came to us this morning. Apparently, you guys might know who this is?"

"Might have an idea."

"Great. It'll save us a ton of work if you do."

They finally reached the room that contained the dead body. They walked inside, seeing the body right in the center of the room on a table. There was a sheet covering the body from head to toe. After they closed the door, Cheryl walked over to the table. Before pulling it off, she glanced back at her two guests.

"You guys ready?"

Recker slightly moved his hands. "Let's do it."

Cheryl pulled the sheet down, stopping once she

reached the man's chest. Both Recker and Haley stepped forward to look at the man more closely. It didn't take long to identify who it was, though. Recker had a solemn expression as he looked at his partner.

"That's the guy," Recker said. "That's the person we're looking for."

"Sorry to hear it," Cheryl replied. "You're sure?"

Recker pulled out his phone and scrolled to a picture of Frank. He showed it to her. She studied the photo, then looked at the face of the dead man.

"Yeah. That looks like him to me."

There wasn't any doubt. Though it looked like Frank had been in the water for a few days, his body was decomposed enough to obscure him totally.

"Friend of yours?" Cheryl asked.

Recker shook his head. "Nope. He worked at a hospital as a security guard. Went missing last week. We were brought in to investigate."

"You guys PI's or something?"

"Something like that."

"You have his information? Name, address, DOB, all that? It'll move everything along faster."

Recker nodded. Once Cheryl grabbed her clipboard, Recker gave her all the information they had on him, which was plenty.

"Foul play, I guess?" Haley asked.

"No," Cheryl answered. "I mean, at least not that I can see right now."

"What? No foul play?"

93

"I've done a brief examination of his body so far. I haven't found anything to indicate anything out of the ordinary. I don't see any needle marks, strangulation marks around his neck, gunshot wounds, nothing. Here, see for yourself."

She took the sheet further down to his waist, letting Recker and Haley have a closer look at the body. But she was right. They didn't see any unusual marks on his body, either. There were no marks around his wrists to indicate he'd been tied up. And as Cheryl suggested, there were no marks of any other kind anywhere on his body.

"It's still possible something could've been done to him," Recker said.

"Sure," she replied. "I mean, he could have some poison in his system, or maybe something else that was injected orally, but as of right now, visually, there's nothing that indicates foul play. But obviously, once we get all the tests back, that could change."

Recker and Haley stood there for a moment, quietly, just staring at the body.

"You guys have that look about you," Cheryl said. "Like you're sure something was done to him. Was he in some sort of trouble?"

"Not that we know of," Recker answered.

"Maybe he just took his own life. Jumped in the river. Unfortunately, we've had quite a few suicide victims lately."

"Really? Like this?"

"Yeah. Actually, this is the fourth body in the last two weeks that has been found in the river."

The woman shrugged. "Who knows? I just analyze the bodies. I don't get into the other stuff."

"Are the police looking into the other ones?"

"Not as far as I know. As of now, all are classified as drownings."

"And you don't think that's strange?"

"Like I said, I just analyze the bodies and report my findings. I don't get paid to investigate the other things. We're extremely understaffed here. I barely have time to do my own job."

"Do you think it's possible you could let me know about Frank's findings once you have them?"

She thought about it for a few seconds. "I guess I could give you a quick rundown."

"And maybe send me the reports on the other three victims that were found?"

Cheryl quickly put her hands up. "Whoa, whoa, whoa. I don't know about all that."

Recker took out one of his business cards and handed it to her. She glanced at it, only seeing a phone number.

"What are you, The Equalizer or something?"

Recker chuckled. "Cute. Not quite."

"All that's on here is a phone number."

"Oh, I forgot."

Recker took the card back and grabbed his pen,

quickly scribbling an email address. He handed the
card back.

"You can send the reports there."

"I could get fired for sending reports to unautho-
rized places."

"I'll authorize it."

"Really?"

"Would it be easier if we come down and pick
it up?"

"No, it wouldn't."

"So what's the best way to go about it, then?"
Recker asked.

"Not at all."

"C'mon, you know Vincent. Do I have to go through
him? You know if I do, I'm gonna see those reports
anyway. Why not just cut out the middleman?"

Cheryl sighed. "You're worse than he is."

"That's kind of hurtful. Look, we don't want to get
you in any kind of trouble. This is just for our own
amusement."

"What is it that you're hoping to find with these
other reports?"

"Honestly? I don't know. Maybe I'll find nothing.
But maybe these are all connected somehow."

"The police don't seem to think so."

"Well, like you, the police are understaffed,"
Recker said. "And sometimes they're pulled in other
directions and just want to close cases before they
should be closed. We're only interested in getting to

the bottom of this. That's all. We have no other agenda. We have no other reason. We just wanna do what's right."

Cheryl looked away for a second. "I can't believe this."

"If it makes you feel better, we can just call Vincent later. I don't want to step on your toes or pressure you or anything."

"Right. Fine. I mean, if the files are on my desk and I'm not here, I can't really stop you from taking pictures of them on your phone or anything, right?"

"Oh, definitely not."

She went over to her file cabinet and took out the files from the previous three suicide victims that were brought in. She placed them on her desk. She then put her hand up to her ear.

"Wait, what's that? I think I'm getting paged somewhere. I'll be back in... three minutes?"

Recker smiled. "Oh, we'll be right here. We won't move an inch."

"Great."

Once Cheryl left the room, Recker and Haley went over to the desk and started going through the folders. They didn't have time to read them now. They just took out their phones and started taking pictures of the information. They'd look at it later. Once they were finished, they closed the folders and went back to their previous positions.

About three minutes after she left, Cheryl

returned. She went over to her desk and picked up the folders.

"Turns out they weren't paging me after all."

"Good to know," Recker replied. "Thank you very much for your time."

"Um, just out of curiosity, do you think you could let me know your findings? I mean, if you figure out that these weren't actually suicides?"

"Yeah. I can do that."

"Thank you."

"Well, I know you're busy, so I guess we'll be getting out of your hair now."

Recker turned to leave, but noticed his partner was staying in place. Haley and Cheryl seemed to be having a flirty glance with each other. Recker grinned, then tapped his partner on the arm.

"You coming?"

Haley shuffled his feet. "Oh. Yeah. Yeah."

"Wait," Cheryl said. "Before you go." She went over to her desk and grabbed a business card, handing it to Haley before he left. "Here's my info if you need to contact me again."

Haley smiled. "Thanks."

"Feel free. Anytime."

Recker put his hand over his mouth to disguise his smile over the situation. "You ready to go?"

Once the two men left the room and went outside, Haley tried to hand over the business card.

"You want this?"

"I'm pretty sure that's for your benefit," Recker answered.

"Well I'm not sure if..."

Recker laughed as they walked along the sidewalk. "Chris, nobody said you had to marry the woman. Call her, talk for a bit, take her out on a date, see what happens. Nothing wrong with that."

"I dunno. It's just with what we do... you know."

"I hear you. But don't make the job your life. I've got Mia. No reason you can't do the same."

Haley looked at the card again. "Maybe."

Recker nudged him in the arm. "Think about it. If you like her, you should do it. She seemed willing. Besides, she somehow knows Vincent. That means she's not oblivious about the life."

Haley laughed. "Knowing Vincent might be a red flag."

"Maybe it is. But like I said, nobody said you had to marry her. Nothing wrong with just going out on a few dates and having a good time."

"Yeah. I'll think about it."

Recker then sighed as they walked to their car.

"What's wrong?"

"I was just thinking about Frank back there," Recker replied.

"Oh. Yeah. It's a shame."

"It is. It's kind of what we initially figured. That don't make it any easier to deal with, though."

"Head back to the office and start putting things together?"

"Not yet. I'll drop you off."

"Where are you going?" Haley asked.

"There's a conversation I need to have first."

"The hospital?"

Recker nodded. "Yeah. We found out what happened to Frank. They should hear it from me."

"That'll be a tough one."

"They always are. I guess it's better than not knowing."

"Better to not know and be alive."

"Yeah. But at least there's closure. Right now, that's the best that I can give them."

11

———

Recker was waiting in the hallway for Mia. She wasn't able to meet him in the cafeteria since she was having a busy day, but she could spare a few minutes. Recker didn't tell her what this was about, as he didn't want to deliver the news in a message or a text. He was leaning against the wall as she came out.

"Hey! This is a nice surprise."

Recker grimaced. "Not that nice."

"What's wrong?"

Recker wasn't one for beating around the bush, and he didn't see the point in doing it here either. He had to just come out with it.

"We found Frank."

There was a fear in Mia's eyes with what she thought she was about to hear. "And?"

"He's dead," Recker solemnly said.

"Oh no. No. Are you sure? How?"

"Yeah, I'm sure. We just saw him at the medical examiner's office."

"You're sure it's him?"

Recker nodded. "It's definitely him."

Mia put her hands on the sides of her face. "I can't believe it."

"I'm sorry."

"What happened?"

"As of right now, they don't suspect foul play."

"They don't? Then how'd he die?"

"Right now, they just think he drowned."

"What?!"

"He was found in the river."

"That can't be right," Mia said. "It can't be."

"I'm just telling you what the initial conclusion is."

"That doesn't make sense."

"I didn't say it made sense," Recker said. "That's just the initial findings."

"There's gotta be more to it."

"Well, I was able to look at the body myself. We couldn't find anything else wrong. There were no other marks on him. No gunshot wounds, no needle marks, no bruises, no strangulation marks, no anything."

"It just doesn't make sense."

"I agree with you. And maybe they'll find something else to suggest he was poisoned, or given something that doesn't show up on the body."

"Does this mean you're done with it?"

Recker shook his head. "No. No, not yet."

By the look on his face, she could tell there was something else. "You do think there's more to it. Don't you?"

"I think there's a lot of suspicious things going on right now. Not just with him."

"Like with what?"

"This is just between us. Nobody else here or anything should know."

"Of course."

"Frank's neighbor turned up dead. When I had that meeting last night, five more people wound up getting killed. And we were told Frank looked like he had a disagreement with someone a few days before he went missing. We don't know who the guy was, though. And the medical examiner told us that three other people had been pulled from the river recently. All presumed to be drowned."

"Seems like a lot of things going on."

"It is," Recker said. "Too many. We're trying to locate the people that killed the five gang members last night. And we're going to start looking into these other drowning victims. See if we can find some type of connection. Something that ties all of this together."

"You think it's all connected?"

Recker shrugged. "What I think and what I can prove are two different things. It feels like there's a connection. I mean, there's a lot of bodies dropping at that one apartment complex lately. That doesn't seem like a coincidence to me. So, we'll keep looking into it, see how it goes."

"I just can't believe that he jumped into the river on his own. Or he fell in. I don't believe it."

"I doubt it, myself. That's why we'll keep digging."

"All right. Well, I should get back in there. Thanks for letting me know. Does anyone else know yet?"

"No. I was going to make a stop at the security office to let Joe know. The police will probably start making notifications soon now that they know who he is, but I figured I'd get a jump on it."

"Thanks." She gave him a quick kiss. "I'll see you later?"

"Yep."

Recker then made his way to the security office to inform Joe. The talk went similarly to the one with Mia, though Recker didn't volunteer anything close to the same amount of information. He left off everything except for finding Frank. That was good enough for him.

Once Recker walked out of the hospital, he sent a text to Haley to let him know he was on his way back to the office.

"Looks like we got some action," Haley texted back.

"What's going on?"

"We got a hit on the car from last night."

"Really? Who's it belong to?"

"David's still trying to run it down. He got the car. Trying to find a good angle of the license plate."

"OK. Should be there soon."

When Recker got to the office, he found Jones and Haley huddled around the computer, obviously looking at something.

"Got our guys yet?" Recker asked.

"Almost," Jones replied. "Just one more small thing."

As he was doing that, Haley pulled up a picture of the car in question on another computer to show his partner.

"This is the shot," Haley said. He pointed to the screen. "See the bullet holes in the door?"

Recker nodded. "Yeah."

"Only problem is, this angle doesn't give a good shot of the plate. So David's trying to see if there's another camera further down the street that can pick it up."

Recker squinted. "How many people are in that car?"

"Looks like four to me. You can see the outlines there."

"It's a good start. Those four people could be anybody, though. We really need something to dive into. A starting point."

"The car doesn't qualify?" Jones asked.

"Not really. It could be any Tom, Dick, or Harry in that thing. We need an actual name."

"I'm working on it."

While he was doing that, Recker remembered the

pictures they took earlier that morning. He pulled out his phone, but just as he and Haley were about to look at them, Jones snapped his fingers, pulling their attention away.

"Was that an important snap?" Recker asked. "Or just a nonchalant one."

"I don't snap unless it's important," Jones replied.

"Oh, you're one of those."

"I've got a plate."

"Nice! Who's it belong to?"

"Doesn't matter. It comes back as stolen. Reported missing three weeks ago."

Recker slapped his leg. "Of course it is."

"Any chance it's a bogus report?" Haley asked.

"Looking into it now," Jones answered. "It doesn't appear that's the case, though. It seems legit."

Recker sighed. "Back to the drawing board."

"Not necessarily."

"What? Why?"

"We may not know who was using that car, but we know where it is now."

"We do?"

"I do. I've got it on the screen now."

"You know where it is right this second?"

"Should I repeat it again? Yes, right this second." Jones pointed to his screen. "It's right there. In the corner."

Recker looked closely, but he didn't recognize the

surroundings. "Where's that? Looks like some type of junkyard."

"I believe that would be accurate."

Jones wrote down the location of the car.

"Are you able to go back and get a picture of the guys as they leave?" Recker asked.

Recker and Haley stood there patiently, hoping they would get a break. It took Jones a few minutes, but he was able to wind the footage back to when the car first arrived. It was about twenty minutes after the incident at the apartments.

"There they are," Haley said, observing the car as it parked.

Recker leaned in, trying to get a better look at their faces. It was dark and blurry, though. And none of them turned around completely to face the camera, which was a good distance away.

"Are we able to zoom in?" Recker asked.

Jones zoomed in on their faces, but they still weren't able to get a clear look at any of the four.

"Is that the best we can do?"

"I'm afraid so," Jones answered. "The camera quality on this isn't the best. It's definitely not a newer model."

"Is it from 1970?"

Jones chuckled. "It may well be."

"Jeez, I mean, come on. We got four guys right there, and we can't do better than this?"

"I can only work with the material that I've got."

"Well I'm not saying it's you, but... c'mon."

"I can see if there's another camera nearby that's got a better look at their faces, but, no guarantees, of course."

"Maybe these guys knew where the camera was," Haley said. "That's why they parked there."

Recker wasn't sure he bought that. "If they knew there was a camera there, they probably wouldn't have parked there at all."

"Yeah, maybe so."

"Probably familiar with the area, though," Jones said. "At least on some level. I'm sure they didn't just park there for no reason."

"Still not helpful, though," Recker said. "How familiar they are with the area doesn't give us anything."

"Well, we've got the car. That's something."

"Yeah, not much. But something."

"You know, those guys might have been in a rush to leave," Haley said. "Now that we know where the car is, maybe we should give it a shakedown."

Recker glanced at his friend and agreed. That had to be the hope now. That one of the four men was sloppy enough to leave some type of evidence behind. But at least now they had the car. Now, they just had to match somebody in it.

12

———————

Recker parked along the street, then he and Haley walked through the front entrance of the business. There were some metal gates, but they were in rough shape, and were never closed. It probably wouldn't close even if they tried. One of the gates appeared to be just barely hanging on to the hinges.

They took a quick look around, but didn't see anyone walking around. There didn't seem to be anything going on there. There was junk and trash everywhere. It didn't look like the place was currently occupied by a business. Unless it was a trash business.

Haley tapped his partner on the arm and pointed to the corner of the property. "There it is."

They walked over to the car, keeping their heads spinning around in case there was someone watching or decided to visit. Haley pulled on the handle of the door and opened it.

"Guess they were too busy to lock it."

"Somehow, I don't think they cared," Recker said.

They started looking inside the car, hoping they would find something that was left behind. A gun, a napkin, something with a name on it, anything they could analyze to figure out who the occupants of the car were. The seats had some trash on it, but nothing they could really use. As Haley checked the glove compartment, Recker started searching underneath the seats. Then Haley began checking the cracks of the seats.

Recker finished his search, not finding anything. Haley could hear his partner's frustration by his loud sigh. Haley wasn't having any better luck. Not at first, anyway. But then, his fingers felt something. It felt like a small piece of paper. It was very thin. He was able to barely grab it with two of his fingers, then pulled it up. He grabbed it with the rest of his hand and looked at it.

"We might have something here."

"What do you got?" Recker asked.

"Fast food receipt."

Recker wasn't impressed. "That's not gonna help."

"You don't think so? I'm not so sure."

"What's that gonna do?"

"Fast-food places have cameras, right?"

"They do."

"And with this receipt, we got the exact time they were there, don't we?" Haley said.

"Assuming it's theirs."

"Date's from yesterday. I think there might be a good chance."

Recker shrugged, still not sure they'd get anything from it. "Worth the shot, I guess."

They spent a few more minutes going over the car. There was nothing else inside that they could find. Then they pulled the trunk open and started going through it. There wasn't anything in there either except for a spare tire. Then, out of the corner of his eye, Haley spotted someone walking over to them.

"Looks like we got company."

Recker removed his head from inside the trunk and stood up straight. "Who's this guy?"

"Head trash man, maybe?"

"Guess we're about to find out."

"Hey!" the man shouted. "What are you guys doing there?"

Neither Recker nor Haley answered. They just stared at him as he got closer.

"What are you guys doing?" the man repeated.

"What's it to you?" Recker asked.

"You can't just be going through things on my property."

"Oh, you own this dump?"

"This might not be the Taj Mahal, but it's still mine. And you got no right to be here going through things."

"Is this your car?"

"No, never seen it before."

"Then what's it doing here?"

"Beats me. You guys cops?"

"We'll ask the questions," Recker said. "If the car's not yours, then you shouldn't object to us looking through it. Right?"

"Uh, I dunno. So you guys are cops? That still don't give you the right to be looking through things without permission."

"This car was involved in a shooting last night. You know anything about that?"

"No."

"Never seen this car before?"

"Never."

"Four men were inside," Haley said. "Know who they were?"

"Well if I don't know the car, I can't know the people inside it either."

"So if you don't know it, why would they leave the car here?"

The man shrugged. "Beats me. How should I know? Apparently anybody can just walk through here and drop things off."

"What exactly do you do here?"

"Mostly deal in metal. Buying and selling."

Recker looked over at the main building and pointed at the camera sitting on the top of it. "You got any other cameras here besides that one?"

"No, that's the only one."

"We don't want you touching this car while it's here. Just in case the owners come back for it."

"What do you mean I can't touch it? What am I supposed to do with it? Just leave it here?"

"That's right," Recker said. "Just leave it."

"It's taking up space. Valuable space."

"Who can tell?" Haley asked.

"Very funny. But I got things coming and going in here all the time. I don't want this junk just sitting here."

"Well that's what you're gonna do," Recker said. "For one, it's stolen. So if you touch it, you'll likely get charged."

"Oh, great! Just great! I don't want no stolen car sitting here! Get it out of here!"

"Want to see if people come back for it first. You'll leave it here for a week. If nobody comes back, then we'll move it."

"Are you kidding me?"

"Nope. And that's what you're gonna do. Or else I'm sure we could look around and find some violations in here."

"You cops. You cops, man. You're all alike."

Recker grinned. "Thanks. So we're gonna keep an eye on this place for the next week. You touch that car, you're getting charged."

The man put his arms up. "Fine, fine. I won't touch it. But one week. I don't want it here no longer than that."

The man walked away, and Recker and Haley turned their attention back to the car. They started to go through it again, making sure they didn't miss something the first time around.

"You think that guy really does know something?" Haley asked.

"I'd say no."

"How are we going to monitor this?"

"David can just keep checking the camera, see if they show up again."

"I'm betting that they won't."

"No bet," Recker said. "They probably left it here because they're not coming back. But, just to be sure, we'll keep an eye on it."

After they were done checking the car again, they started to leave. Haley held up the receipt.

"Looks like this is all we got to work on right now."

"Yeah," Recker said. "Let's hope that's enough."

"We've got enough things going on right now that one of them should start paying dividends."

"You think so?"

"We got the receipt. We got the car, so David can keep checking cameras for other days, see if one of them gives us a clear picture of one of the passengers. And we still got those reports from the medical examiner to look over. With all of that, something's gotta break for us."

Recker chuckled. "I like your optimism. Not sure if it's warranted, but I like it."

Haley joined in the laughter. "Don't worry. There's enough of that to go around."

"Maybe you'll be so optimistic, you will it into being true."

"Maybe so."

"Let's head back to the office and see if we can put your optimism to good use."

"I predict one of these things will work for us. At least one."

"You're into predictions now, are you?"

"If that's what it takes."

"I don't know if you're right," Recker said. He then put his fingers in the air. "But I'll cross my fingers."

"We got a lucky rabbit's foot too? Might as well pull out all the stops."

"Whatever it takes. Maybe on the way back we can stop and get all the lucky whatever's we can find. Because right now, I'm willing to do just about anything."

13

Once Recker and Haley got back to the office, they first peppered Jones with some questions about his progress. Or lack thereof.

"How are you making out?" Recker asked.

"Well, considering I didn't reach out to you, that should tell you the answer right there."

"Nothing?"

"Not a thing," Jones answered. "For the moment. You know how things go, though. It can change on a dime."

"I'd take a nickel right now."

"Let's take a look at those records," Haley said.

Recker and Haley gave Jones their phones.

"Can you put the records up there on the big screen?" Recker asked. "Might be easier if we all see them at the same time."

Jones took their phones and within a minute, the

pictures were up on the screen on the wall. It started with Frank's, though his wasn't final. But considering they looked at him, they didn't need a final report. The one they had was good enough.

"What exactly are we looking for?" Jones asked.

"I'll let you know if I see it."

"See what?"

"I don't know. That's what I'm looking for."

"For what?"

"Something to jump out at me," Recker replied.

"So we're looking for the needle in the haystack?"

"I'll take a thimble."

"How reassuring."

Once they were done looking at Frank's report, they moved along to the next victim. And they kept going until they had looked at all four. Nothing initially jumped out at them as suspicious. It could have all been legit. Maybe there was nothing strange or nefarious about any of it. But Recker just couldn't shake the feeling that something was going on.

They started at the beginning again, going over every single thing in detail. Nothing was tossed aside without some thought given to it.

"Frank was the only one not identified," Jones said.

"At first," Recker replied. "Remember, he was just found this morning. Given a few more days, he probably would have been identified without us."

"True."

"All found in the river," Haley said. "No marks on any of the bodies."

"Kind of strange."

Jones was able to pull up all the reports and put them side by side. Recker and Haley moved closer to the screen to inspect all of them. Recker's eyes kept dancing between the four reports. There was something there. There had to be. He just wasn't seeing it yet.

"All four victims were over fifty," Haley said.

"Three men and one woman," Recker continued.

"Two were single, two were not."

"Can we look up their professions?"

"I'm on it," Jones replied.

"There's gotta be something else here."

"It's their addresses," Haley said. "Look at them. All four live close to each other."

"All within a couple miles. Why is that significant?"

"Excuse me?" Jones said.

"I mean, I know why it's significant. But, why would they all live so close to each other? What could they have done?"

"Or what did they see?" Haley asked.

"You're both assuming that they saw or did something," Jones said. "There is always the possibility, no matter how small or remote, that they all really did die of natural causes."

"Drowning in a river is not natural."

"You know what I mean. It wasn't of someone else's doing. Is that better?"

"Not really," Recker replied. "They're all still dead."

"Let's put them on the map," Haley said.

He walked around the desk and sat down at the computer, putting in all four addresses of the deceased. Once he did, he raised his eyebrows.

"That's pretty close."

Recker came around to look, standing over his partner's shoulder. He pointed to one of the addresses.

"That one's literally across the street from Frank."

Haley nodded. "And this one is two minutes up the street."

"The last one is one block over."

"I don't know. That's a little fishy to me. And I know you don't believe in coincidences."

"So what did all these people run into that got them killed?"

"Allegedly," Jones said. "There is still no evidence they were murdered."

Recker casually glanced at his friend, though he didn't reply, or give it much thought. He didn't need evidence to know it. There was no way four random people, all living in the same area, just happened to take a plunge in the river without being forced. Or thrown in there after being killed.

"This isn't natural. They ran into something, or more likely, someone, that didn't like what they were doing."

"Such as?" Jones asked.

Recker threw his hands up. "I don't know. Maybe there's a rival gang rolling in."

"That your friend T-Bone doesn't know about? Highly unlikely, I would think."

"And how's that match up with Jamar?" Haley asked. "He was killed in a completely different manner than the others."

"As well as the gang members."

Recker sat down and put his hand on his face as he thought about it. "The initial four were all killed in the same way. All supposedly drowned. The others weren't killed until we showed up. And they were shot."

"Though Jamar was made to look like a suicide as well."

"The question is why? What do all these people have in common?"

"I can't answer that, but I can shed some light on a few other things," Jones said. "We know Frank was a security guard at the hospital. One of the other victims drove a bus. One was a retired school teacher. And the other drove a taxi."

"What connection do they all have to each other?" Recker asked himself.

Haley started thinking out loud. "Bus. Taxi. Transportation."

"What's that got to do with a school teacher and security guard?"

"Maybe nothing. Maybe it's not connected like we think."

Jones jumped in. "All, in their own way, are doing some sort of public service. Teaching. Public transportation. Security work."

Recker started nodding. "Yeah. Could be."

"But what would get them killed?" Haley asked.

"I don't know. But the odds of them all getting depressed within weeks of each other and throwing themselves in the river seem extremely low to me."

"So what did they see, or hear, that got themselves into trouble?" Jones asked.

"It has to be a rival gang," Recker said. "I don't see what else it could be."

"If that's the case, why target these people?" Haley said. "I mean, T-Bone's men, sure, I can understand that. But why the others? And drowning people isn't exactly any gang's MO that I can think of."

"That's a good point," Jones replied. "Gang's usually come in with authority. They usually want people to know they're around to start causing fear and panic."

Recker put his hand on his head. "This doesn't make any sense."

"You're also going under the assumption that this is all somehow related. Maybe it's not. Maybe it's just as random and nonsensical as it appears."

"That's hard to believe."

"I know. But random occurrences, and coincidences, do occur on occasion."

"Not when I'm around."

"It's something that needs to be given weight to, no matter your stance on the subject. It does exist. Especially if we cannot find any other links to these people."

"We need to dig deep on this," Recker said. "A lot further. There's some kind of connection to these people. We just can't see it yet. But I'm sure it's there. Has to be."

"Has to be or hope to be?"

"Both. I can't accept that this is all some random incident. Life doesn't work that way."

"Random happens all the time, Michael."

"But not when we're involved."

Jones raised an eyebrow. He thought this might have been one of those times where they overstepped. Still, he wasn't going to fight and argue just yet. There was still more work to be done. In these types of cases, things didn't always just bubble to the top. Sometimes, as Recker suggested, a lot of digging had to be done. And that would take some time. But once they did the work, if nothing came of it, then Jones would be more forceful in his assertion that this might all be nothing more than a coincidence. But the time for that claim wasn't now. Now, they had to dig. And hope that something was unearthed.

14

Several days had passed. The team kept digging, though up to that point, nothing was uncovered that led to any sort of light being placed on the matter. They were as much in the dark as they had been. They put out feelers, met with T-Bone again, everything they could think of to try to get a lead. Nothing was panning out, though.

Recker and Haley were out all morning, trying to run things down. But after striking out, they were ready to head back to the office.

"Let's grab some lunch," Haley said. "Take it back to the barn. Figure out where to go from here."

"Yeah, might as well."

They grabbed some fast food, picking up something for Jones as well. Once they got back to the office, they all started digging in. Jones cleared his throat as if he had something to say. The other two looked at him.

"What was that?" Recker asked.

Jones cleared his throat again. "That?"

"Yes, that. What was it for?"

"Sometimes a throat just needs to be cleared."

"No, not when you do it. You always say I have my tics. Facial expressions, pacing around, things like that."

"And you do."

"Yeah, well, so do you. Sometimes you do that throat-clearing thing when you have something on your mind that you're not quite sure how to say."

"I do not," Jones said, looking at their other partner.

Haley confirmed it, though. "Yeah, you kind of do."

"Oh. Well I should be more mindful of it in the future."

"You do that," Recker said. "But how about you spill what's on your mind now?"

"Well I don't have everything clear yet."

"We work all the time with things not being clear. I don't mind wading through the mud here."

Jones ate a handful of fries before continuing. "I've gone back a long way here. A long way."

"OK?"

"It turns out that twenty years ago, Frank and his wife tried fostering."

"Like... kids?"

"What other kind of fostering is there?"

"Dogs?"

Jones rolled his eyes. "Really, Michael?"

Recker shrugged. "Just saying."

"Yes, kids. I was able to get the records from the state."

"I'm assuming that plays into what we're looking at somehow?"

"Yes, Michael, it does. If you let me go on, you'll see how."

"Oh, good. Continue."

"Thanks. Anyway, as I was saying, Frank and his wife fostered a couple of children. But only three."

"Fostering's not for everyone."

"Apparently there was this one child who was particularly troublesome. William Addison. Records indicate a lot of problems with him."

"What kind of problems?"

"You know, not listening, getting into trouble, sneaking out, that sort of thing."

"How old was he?" Recker asked.

"Twelve at the time."

"I'm assuming this somehow plays into our current predicament?"

"I'm getting to it."

"Oh, OK. It's one of those long stories, huh?"

Jones ignored him, then continued on. "Anyway, I did some checking on the three foster children they had. The other two were older than Addison. They were fifteen and sixteen."

"Are they involved in this somehow?"

"The older two? No, not that I can see. They appear to have gone on to bigger and better things. One's a doctor, the other started his own business."

"And Addison?"

"Constant trouble with the law over the last twenty years, particularly the last fifteen, once he reached seventeen."

"And what, you think this guy killed his foster parent?" Recker asked.

Jones raised an eyebrow, indicating that was exactly what he was thinking. "Well..."

"Wait, you do?"

"In doing a search on Addison, several other interesting things came to light."

"Such as?"

Jones reached back on his desk and grabbed a paper, handing it to Jones. "See anything interesting on there?"

Recker's eyes immediately went to a name that was highlighted. "You kind of gave it away there."

"Just wanted to make it stand out."

Recker recognized the name immediately. It was the name of the school teacher that was killed.

"What's the connection?"

"She was one of Addison's teachers."

"Really? Wow. So he killed his foster father, and his teacher. What's he on, a revenge kick?"

"Possibly."

"This doesn't prove he killed them, though," Haley

said. "Just because he knows them both doesn't indicate he harmed them."

Jones put his finger in the air. "I'm getting to that. You'll change your mind when you hear the rest. The bus driver was a youth sports coach. He did it all. Basketball, baseball, football, everything. Addison was enrolled in the program for two years at the ages of fifteen and sixteen."

"Connection number three," Recker said.

"I don't have any concrete information about him having trouble there, but I'm willing to bet that Addison clashed with the coach."

"Still speculation," Haley said. "Why am I taking up the David role, by the way?"

The others laughed.

"Somebody has to," Recker said.

"What about the taxi driver?" Haley asked.

"I've saved the best for last," Jones replied. "The taxi driver is Addison's real father."

Both Recker and Haley seemed speechless. They had stunned looks on their faces, and in Haley's case, his mouth fell open.

"Say what?" Haley asked.

Jones nodded. "The taxi driver is Addison's biological father."

"That's a four-for-four," Recker said. "Sounds pretty slam dunk to me."

"Wait a minute," Haley said. "The taxi driver's last name isn't Addison."

"He took on his mother's last name," Jones replied.

"So why was Addison in foster care, then?"

"His father had severe drug issues. In and out of jail constantly."

"Where's the mother? How do we know she's not next on the list? Or if he already got to her?"

"It's not a concern," Jones answered. "His mother died when he was twelve. That was actually what put him in foster care to begin with."

The trio continued talking and throwing theories into the air for the next few minutes.

"What I don't get is why he waited so long?" Haley asked. "If he's got a problem with all these people, why did he wait twenty years?"

"Well, it's actually not as long as that," Jones replied. "It's more or less the last fourteen, since he reached eighteen."

"Still, the point's the same. A lot of time between then and now."

"A good reason for that. He's been in and out of jail and rehab multiple times over the last fourteen years."

"But what made him snap now? Why not kill them between jail stints five years ago, if that's what he was planning?"

Recker tilted his head up, closed his eyes, and rubbed his throat as he thought about it. "Because it wasn't planned."

"What?"

"He didn't plan to do this. I don't think."

"How do you figure that?" Haley asked. "He just killed four people on accident?"

"Because you're right. If he was angry at them, he could've killed them long ago. And think about what we know so far. I'm willing to bet he was the one that T-Bone saw talking to Frank."

"It was heated, apparently."

"It was. And there was the conversation at Frank's apartment too, that Jamar overheard."

"Seems to be supporting my case."

"But it's not," Recker said. "If Addison was angry at him, he could've killed him before that. But they kept seeing each other. Why?"

Haley snapped his fingers, starting to see his point. "Yeah, yeah, yeah. And didn't Jamar say he heard Frank say something like, 'I've tried to help you' or something like that?"

"Yeah. That would fit. Maybe he was going to all these people for help, and for whatever reason, they weren't giving it to him."

"Or he just thought they weren't giving it to him."

"Either way amounts to the same thing. Addison went to them for help because he knew them. And they either couldn't help him, or wouldn't, or didn't help him in the way that he wanted."

"And then he lashed out."

Recker nodded. "That would fit."

"But the gang members and Jamar?" Jones asked.

"How do they fit in? I see nothing that connects any of them up to this point."

"I don't know. Maybe it's a coincidence."

Jones looked shocked. "What? Do my ears deceive me? Did you actually just say that something might be a coincidence?"

"Yeah, I said maybe. Or maybe we just haven't found the reason yet. I'm sure there must be one."

"Don't forget, they were killed in a different manner," Haley said. "The reason might be that it's not connected at all and we just stumbled into a different thing altogether."

"Could be it."

"Maybe we should just put those things aside for the moment," Jones said. "Investigate these things as two separate incidents until we can actually prove that they are related."

Recker took a final bite of his cheeseburger as he thought about it. "Well, we're in this to find out what happened to Frank. That's where we direct our efforts first. The gang thing is T-Bone's problem."

"Unless it's connected to Frank in some way that we don't see as of yet."

"Yeah. But Frank is our first priority. And finding Addison... that's our next one."

15

Haley walked up to the Medical Examiner Office building, finding Cheryl waiting outside for him. She called a little earlier, asking for Recker and Haley to come down. Recker was working on finding William Addison, so Haley made the trip alone. She smiled when she saw Haley approach.

"Nice to see you again."

Haley returned the smile. "You too."

"Where's your partner?"

"Oh, he's, uh, a little busy right now."

"So you're riding solo, huh?"

"For the moment. You have something for us?"

"Let's go inside and have a chat."

Haley nodded and followed Cheryl inside the building. They went to a regular office this time, no dead bodies in sight. It was pretty small, and looked a little disorganized, with stuff on the floor, next to the file cabinet, and all across the desk.

"Excuse the mess," Cheryl said, trying to tidy up her desk on the fly. "Things are pretty crazy right now."

"No worries."

"I'm really not as disorganized as it looks."

"You really don't have to do anything for me. I know you're busy."

Cheryl looked at him and smiled, then looked up and blew her blonde hair out of her face. She sighed and rubbed her eyes.

"Putting in some long days?"

"You have no idea," she replied. "Like, fifteen-hour days. We're shorthanded, and they refuse to hire more people because they say they don't have the money." She put her hands up for air quotes. "Sure. No money. Right. Like every other business. They just wanna do more with less. God forbid you don't work your employees into the ground." She put her hand on her forehead. "I'm sorry. I'm rambling and venting."

Haley smiled. "No, it's all good. Rant away. I'm a good listener. We all gotta get it out sometimes."

"Do you ever have those moments when you just wanna say 'screw it all', and just walk out and never come back?"

"Yeah, I think everyone has those moments at times."

"Well I'm just about there."

"Sounds like you need a night out to blow off some steam or something."

"I could really use it. Are you offering?"

The question took Haley by surprise. "Am I offering? Uh... um..."

Cheryl let out a small laugh. "No, I'm just kidding. Don't, uh... how about we get into why I called you?"

"Sounds good."

"So, we got toxicology reports back on three of our suicide victims. The only one we don't have back yet is Frank, because, well, it's too soon for his."

"I understand."

"So, anyway, the reports indicate that all three of the victims did die by drowning."

"Really?" Haley was surprised by the news. "I really thought there would be something else."

"Well, I'm getting to that. They all died by drowning. But they didn't die in the river."

"What?"

Cheryl grinned, seeing the confused look on Haley's face. "I know, right?"

"Then where did they drown?"

"I believe in a swimming pool."

"What?"

"I know. Crazy. But in all three victims, there was evidence of chlorine. Now, I'm no genius or anything, but I'm pretty sure there's no chlorine in the river. In addition to that, each of the victims showed evidence of a drug. The same drug. And it's used for sedation."

"Sedation? So... he basically knocked them out?"

"Who's he? You know who did it?"

Haley cleared his throat, realizing he let something slip that wasn't intended. "Uh, well, we have a suspect in mind, yeah."

"Who is it?"

Haley slightly turned his head and scratched the back of it. "Well..."

"Oh, come on, I'm giving you all this info. You can at least give me something too."

"Yeah, we found a connection to all four victims. One guy's name came up."

"Well I'm glad for that." Cheryl put her hand on her forehead, looking like she lost her train of thought. "Um, yeah, what was I saying?"

"The sedation?"

"Oh yeah. Anyway, um, they were basically knocked out before drowning. And it must've been something they took orally, because, as I noted earlier, there were no marks on the body to indicate a needle or anything."

"So this guy drugged them, then drowned them in a swimming pool?"

"That's about the size of it."

"Then, what, took them down to the river and threw them in?"

"I would guess so."

"Why?"

Cheryl shrugged. "I don't know. Not really my

department. Guess he thought they'd stay under. Or he assumed that people would think they jumped in the river and killed themselves."

"Not very bright. Didn't he think there'd be testing done?"

"I'll be honest, I don't think most people understand what can be detected these days."

"Probably not."

"So I'm gonna send all this to the police with my findings. Do you want me to send the name of your suspect along?"

"Uh, no, I'd really prefer you pretend like I was never here," Haley answered.

Chery's shoulders dropped, like there was something else on her mind. "Who are you guys? Really. I mean, you're very secretive, and it's not really natural to be like that."

Haley smiled. "Can't really tell you."

"Please tell me you're not criminals or something, because no matter how much I dislike this job sometimes, it's still... well, you know."

"Relax. We're not criminals. We're here to help."

"But how? Because you know Vincent, and I know what Vincent is, so if you know and work with him, then that gives me a pretty good idea about who you are."

Haley shook his head. "We don't work with Vincent. Well, we kind of do sometimes, but we're not employed by him."

"Great. So you're a different gang?"

"No, we're not a gang. We're just... wait a minute, you know Vincent. I could say the same about you. How do I know you're not a criminal?"

"Excuse me? I work here."

"I know where you work," Haley said. "But there's plenty of people who work in respectable positions, but do some questionable things on the side."

"So now you're saying I do questionable things on the side?"

"Well you know Vincent too."

Cheryl was starting to get heated and pointed her finger at him. She was about to unload, but then took a few seconds and thought about it.

"You're right. You're right. I can't really argue." She folded her arms. "Tell you what. I'll tell you my story if you tell me yours. Deal?"

Haley titled his head back and rubbed his neck. He knew he shouldn't agree. It really didn't matter. But he did anyway. "Deal."

Cheryl leaned forward, putting her elbows on the desk. "Where to begin? So, my father was... not a great person. In fact, he was kind of an ass. But anyway, he, in some sort of fashion, knew Vincent or did work for him, or owed him money, I'm not really sure. I really don't wanna know anything about that kind of stuff. Anyway, long story short, Vincent paid for me to get through school."

"Really?"

"After high school, I wasn't going to be able to afford college, even with scholarships and loans. It was just going to be too much. Plus, I was working on the side to help my mother with bills, because... my dad was an ass and all and barely paid for anything. So I was just going to skip college and work full-time."

"Then Vincent came along?"

Cheryl nodded. "I guess he somehow found out what the situation was. I don't know why he chose to do it. But he paid for my schooling, and paid for some of my mother's bills, so we didn't have to worry about it, and I only had to work a part-time job around my classes."

"And in return?"

"Well, I didn't find this part out until after I was done, that he'd appreciate it if I could pass on any information I could if there was something here that needed to be looked into."

"There it is. Vincent always has a source and a connection somewhere."

Cheryl faked a smile. "That would be me."

"How many times does he need that favor repaid?"

"Actually, not as much as I feared. A couple times a year. And he doesn't ask me to do anything unethical or whatever. Just answer whatever questions he has. Well, I guess giving away this information is unethical, and I'd get fired for it if anyone found out, but it is what it is."

"Don't worry. I'm sure if that ever happened,

Vincent has a connection above you to make sure it doesn't."

"Wouldn't surprise me. So what's your story? How are you indebted to him?"

"I'm not. Mike and I do our own thing."

"Oh, your partner's name is Mike? How nice."

Haley put his hand over his mouth for a moment. "Man. I got some loose lips today."

Cheryl laughed. "It's really OK. Whatever you do, I'm not really in a position to tell anyone, am I?"

"I guess not."

"So what's your name?"

"Chris. And Mike and I just go out and try to help people. I guess it's not always technically legal. But we're trying to make the city a better place. Anyway, that's our story."

"That's a pretty short story."

"That's pretty much all I got."

Cheryl wasn't satisfied with that answer and kept pestering him with more questions. Haley artfully dodged most of them. But eventually, he let a few cracks show and wore down.

"Fine. But this is the last piece of information I'll give you. Some people call us The Silencers."

Cheryl's eyes opened wide. She'd heard of them before. "Are you kidding?!"

"No. Why?"

"I've heard so much about you guys already. Do

you know the six and nine are right around the corner?"

Haley smiled. "I'm aware."

"I've heard those guys talking so many times about you guys."

"Everything good, I hope?"

Cheryl grimaced and shook her hand in the air. "Eh, fifty-fifty. Some like and appreciate you and some don't."

"Seems to be about normal."

"Wow. And you guys are here in my office. So cool."

"I guess you're not one of the ones that wants to throw us in jail?"

Cheryl put her hands up. "Hey, who am I to say what other people should do? I just stay in my own little world, examining people. You do you."

Haley stood up. "Well, I guess that's it for our session."

"Oh, wait."

"You have something else?"

"Um, no, not really. I... don't really know why I said that. I guess it's just the exhaustion speaking."

"You should really do something about that. You're no good to anyone if you run yourself into the ground."

Cheryl lifted up the folders and let them fall back to the desk. "Yeah. Eventually."

"You need to just cut things off at five, then go out, have a drink, have a piece of pizza, whatever, just clear your mind and have a good time, leaving this place behind."

"Sounds perfect. If you know of anyone, send them my way."

"Maybe... someone's here?"

Cheryl squinted one of her eyes. "Are you asking me out?"

"Uh, maybe?"

"Cause if you are, I would totally say yes!"

Haley grinned. "Then I guess I am."

"I'm excited. I can't wait."

"Just so you know, we have a schedule where things come up very suddenly sometimes."

"I'm flexible. Whatever works for you."

"I guess I'll call you later? And just so you know, I'm not a very fancy kind of guy."

Cheryl smiled. "I love pizza! I don't need fancier than that."

"All right. Well, I guess I'll see you later, then."

"You will."

They bid each other goodbye, then Haley left the building. Once he was outside, he looked up at the sky. "Not a bad day." He then sent Recker a message. *"Looks like we're in business."*

16

Once Haley got back to the office, he immediately tried to tell the others what was going on. Recker had other things on his mind, though. There was a reason he let Haley go there by himself. And it wasn't because Recker was too busy.

"So how'd it go?"

"It went good," Haley replied. "Like I told you, I got the information on those other victims."

Recker put his hand out to stop him from going any further. "Yeah, I know. But, before we get into that, what about the other thing?"

Haley looked lost. "What other thing?"

"You know. You and Cheryl. That thing."

Jones' ears suddenly perked up. "Who? What? Cheryl, who? What's going on?"

Recker chuckled. "Chris and Cheryl were giving each other flirty glances when we checked on Frank."

"We were not!" Haley said.

"That's not what I saw."

"Oh, please," Jones said. "Don't tell me we're going to have to deal with another one of these situations."

"What situations?!" Haley asked.

"You know, like Mike had with Mia for a long time. Will he, won't he, maybe, yes, no, I think, ugh... he was worse than a teenage boy pining over his first crush."

"I was not!" Recker replied.

"That's how I remember it."

"I think your memory's starting to fail you, then."

Jones shook his head and pointed at the side of his temple. "Still sharp as a tack."

Haley instantly tried to shut down any worries. "There is no pining going on. There's nothing happening. We just agreed to go out for pizza. That's all."

Recker laughed and slapped his leg. "Ah, so you did ask her!"

"Well, it was kind of like a mutual thing. There was no..."

Jones put his hand on his forehead. "Good Lord. We're gonna do this again."

"There's nothing to worry about. Nothing's happening."

"Yet!" Recker said.

"It's just one date."

"You can't have a second without a first."

"I've been fretting about this day," Jones said.

"There's nothing to worry about," Haley replied. "It's just one day. And pizza. Nothing fancy."

"Doesn't have to be fancy," Recker said. "It's the action."

"There's no action. It's just me going out for pizza with someone."

"On a date."

"Well, I wouldn't call it a date. It's just, uh..."

"What would you call it? You and a strange person going out together for food. Most people call that a date."

"No. It's just a... a..."

"Yes?"

"It's just a... you know... a... get-together."

"It's a date."

Haley rolled his eyes. "Can we get off this subject now?"

"Oh, Chris," Jones said.

"What?!"

"I hope you don't fall into that same trap that Mike did. That was brutal for a while."

"So you keep saying."

"It wasn't that bad," Recker said.

"You didn't have to put up with you," Jones said. "Well, you know what I mean."

Haley was hoping to end the conversation. "I appreciate the concern. But it's just one... outing. I'm not falling head over heels for somebody. We're not dating. I'm barely even giving it a second thought.

We're just going out for pizza. That's it. There's no guarantee we'll even see each other again after this."

"Is she married?"

Haley gave him a look.

"I don't mean now. I mean... ex."

"I don't know."

"Have kids?"

"I don't know. And before you keep on with the questions, I'll answer for any others you might have in mind. I don't know. I don't know much about her. I guess we'll have something to talk about over pizza."

"Does she know who you are?" Jones asked.

"Uh, yeah."

"Wait, what?" Recker said. "She does?"

"I might have let it slip," Haley answered. "We were talking about her Vincent connection, and she said she'd tell me if I told her my background."

"Well you didn't have to be honest," Jones said.

"We're supposed to be the good guys, right? Be honest. Tell the truth. All that."

"Well we're not supposed to be advertising our presence either."

"It's fine. She was fine with it. No problems there."

"So you think. What if you go to this pizza place later and there's a line of police officers outside waiting for you?"

"I don't think that'll happen," Haley replied.

"But you can't say for sure."

"David, I'm sure it's fine," Recker said. "Even if that

did happen, Lawson still owes us a favor. But Vincent knows this woman. I'm sure he'd pull some strings."

"I just always advocate on the side of caution."

"We know. Speaking of which, how does she know Vincent? Did she say?"

Haley nodded. "She did. Something about her father was the one who really knew Vincent. She doesn't really know him except for him calling once or twice a year for a favor. He put her through school."

"Really?"

"That's what I said."

"Interesting."

"Yeah. Anyway, can we move on to another topic? I'm kind of exhausted already."

"What about the other victims?" Jones asked.

Haley then told them the findings that Cheryl gave him. They sat there kind of stunned. It wasn't exactly the news that they were expecting.

"A swimming pool?" Jones said.

"That's right," Haley responded.

"This kind of goes against what we were thinking, then."

"How so?"

"I mean, all of them being drowned in the river is one thing. This is something else. This is serial killer tendencies. This isn't meeting these people down by the river, getting mad, then strangling them there and throwing them in. This is another level."

Recker agreed. "There's the purchase of the drugs

needed to sedate them. Multiple. Then taking them to wherever this swimming pool is. Killing them there. Then transporting them to the river and throwing them in. That's a lot of planning."

"But why? Why is he snapping at these people that have tried to help him over the years?"

"But did they?" Haley asked. "I'm just thinking in Addison's mind here. What if he blamed his father for his mother's death? Or being in foster care? And we don't know about that teacher. Maybe she was extra hard on him. Same for the sports coach. Maybe Addison didn't play much, or got cut from a team, or got yelled at a lot. We don't know they tried to help him."

"And Frank?" Jones asked.

"His friends and coworkers say he was a good guy. We don't know what kind of foster father he was. And maybe he was great. Maybe Addison was just someone that couldn't be helped. But I'm not sure we should follow the narrative that all these people tried to help him. We don't know that."

"That's a good point," Recker said. "The two times we know Frank and Addison were together, they were arguing."

"But they were given a drug," Jones said. "Presumably, he gave it to them. Why would they willingly take something from someone they were having problems with?"

"Maybe he offered them a drink? Presented it as

something to make peace with. Something to put their past issues behind them? I'm just spitballing. I don't know. I don't know if we'll ever know. But I do know we gotta find this guy before he keeps going. He's already killed four. Most people like him don't stop. They'll keep going."

Jones pointed to his computer. "On that end, I've had no luck finding him. There are a couple addresses associated with him, but he's not living at any of them currently. In fact, I can't find him living anywhere for longer than five or six months at a time."

"Somebody's gotta know him. Even if they don't know where he's living, he's gotta be known by somebody. Those drugs he's giving people don't supply themselves."

Haley snapped his fingers. "That's it. That's our next step. Let's figure out who the biggest suppliers are of that drug, work our way backwards. One of them will definitely know him."

"Do you know what drug it was?"

Haley pulled out his phone. "Yeah, she told me the name of it."

Recker took out his phone right after it.

"What are you doing?" Jones asked.

"Well, we all know who's going to be the one to know the biggest suppliers and where they can be located. Right?"

"I suppose so. But don't you want to wait until I can see if I can run it down first?"

"This guy's killed four people already that we know of. Do you really want to take the chance of giving him more time to do it again?"

"We don't know that he's continuing."

"We don't know that he's not either," Recker replied. "And I don't know about you, but I really don't want to give him extra chances to keep it going. Let's find him as soon as possible before he's got another chance to put someone in the river. That's all that matters right now. Just finding him. Nothing else comes close."

17

Recker had arranged a meeting with Vincent, hoping to get the names of a few suppliers they could have a chat with. But there was still some time to kill until then. For now, they were just waiting in the office until it was time to go.

Jones still had his hands full, though, juggling multiple things. One of those things was still looking into the murders of T-Bone's men. Even though at this point, they weren't sure if it was connected to Frank, or Addison, they couldn't definitely rule it out yet.

"Looks like I've got a hit," Jones said.

Both Recker and Haley scurried over to him.

"On what?" Recker asked.

"I've tapped into the camera footage at the fast-food restaurant."

Jones brought up the picture on the big screen on the wall. As Recker looked at it, it wasn't as promising as he hoped. While there was one person on the screen, and his face was very visible, the others in the car weren't so clear. It was obvious that there were four people in the car, so it didn't look like they were going to make out anyone except the driver. But, they did have the driver, so it wasn't all bad. Just not as great as he hoped.

"Just got the one," Recker said.

"That's enough to get started," Jones replied. "Once we have the one, the others will follow soon enough. Guilt by association."

"How long will it take before we have this guy's info?" Haley asked.

"Already running it through the facial rec software as we speak. I don't suspect it will take too long. It's a pretty clear shot of him."

Recker looked at the time, counting down the minutes until his meeting.

"Depending on how this goes, how shall we play this?" Jones asked.

"I don't follow," Recker replied.

"If this is somehow related to Addison, obviously it rolls right into everything. It doesn't really change much. But if it isn't related to Addison, do we just let it go?"

"Not much use in speculating before we have the facts."

"I suppose not. But it would be helpful to start

thinking about plans and actions so we can be prepared with whatever the result might be."

"I don't know about you, but even if it isn't related to Addison, I don't think we can just let it go," Haley said.

"Why?" Jones asked.

"Even if this is just another gang rolling in, there's a lot of people in this area. Some good people. Kids, teenagers, seniors, take your pick. I think they deserve to try and live without the fear of getting shot or having drugs all over the place."

Recker nodded, agreeing with every word. He let out a subtle smile. "And that's why I said there's no use in speculating. We're going to take care of them, whatever the result is."

"Even though it's gang against gang?" Jones asked. "Presumably, that is."

"I think Chris pretty much laid it out perfectly. It's not to avenge any gang killings. It's to prevent future bad things from happening there. That's our mission, is it not? To prevent bad things from happening to good people?"

"And T-Bone? How does he fit in?"

Recker shrugged, barely giving him a second thought. "He doesn't."

"His gang isn't eliminated. He still remains."

"We'll just have to see how it goes."

"He'll recruit more. We'll temporarily eliminate the

problem only to see it resurface in three months when we're preoccupied with something else."

"All we can do is live in the moment. What happens in three months, or six months, we'll have to deal with it at that time if it comes up."

They waited about half an hour, and then they got the alert. They system hit a match.

"Let's see what this says," Jones said. "Ninety percent match. This is our guy."

He brought up the picture of the man, comparing it to what they had on the video. It sure looked like the same guy to them. They briefly looked over his information, though they didn't get a chance for a full rundown yet.

"Listen, we're gonna get going for the meeting with Vincent," Recker said.

Jones nodded. "I'll break everything down with this guy, find out his history, who he associates with. Hopefully by the time you get back, I'll have more for you."

Recker patted his friend on the back. "Sounds like a plan."

Recker and Haley then left, going to a park to meet Vincent. It wasn't one of the more popular parks, with not many people ever visiting, and there wasn't much to do except walk around for the nature lovers. They found Vincent sitting on a bench, feeding some ducks.

They approached him, slipping through his guards, and wading through the ducks to sit on the bench next to him. Vincent looked at the both of them.

"Oh, no. I got double trouble today," he said with a laugh.

"Figured I'd bring some backup," Recker replied. He looked at the dozens of ducks around. "Didn't realize you were going to be surrounded, though."

Vincent laughed. "Yeah. Just one of the things that keeps me relaxed sometimes."

"Pretty sure I saw a sign that said not to feed the ducks," Haley said. "You're living dangerously."

"Yeah. I saw that too. Figured it didn't apply to me. I mean, who cares if I feed some ducks? Would they prefer me to come in here with a shotgun and try to cook a few of them? Besides, they look hungry." He pointed to one of the ducks in front. "Look at that guy. Looks like he's starving. Probably hasn't eaten in weeks."

He reached into his brown bag and tossed a few bread crumbs down.

"Never pictured you as a duck guy," Recker said.

Vincent chuckled. "We all have our secrets, Mike. We all have our secrets." He held the bag open for his guests. "Care to partake?"

Both Recker and Haley reached in, grabbing a handful. They both threw their crumbs down for their hungry friends.

"Soothing, isn't it?" Vincent said.

"Sure," Recker answered. He didn't seem as relaxed as his counterpart. He didn't seem interested in staying very long, either. "Anyway, about that list of names. Did you get a chance to run it down?"

Vincent reached into his pocket and removed a folded piece of paper. "I did."

He handed it to Recker, who immediately unfolded it and read it.

"Four names?"

Vincent nodded. "Those are the guys you'd be looking for."

"You're sure? Nobody else?"

Vincent threw his left hand up. "Sure, there could always be a new guy out there, a new player, someone we haven't identified yet. That's always a possibility. But the drug you're talking about isn't exactly on the top ten bestseller list. It's a small group of guys that deal in stuff like that. You're talking about real dangerous stuff in the hands of the wrong people. And it's not stuff most people can grow in their backyard. This takes some connections to get this stuff."

Recker looked at the list. "Any of these more likely than the others?"

"I put them in order of most likely. I think one is your best bet. But if not, it could easily be any of the other three."

"You deal with any of them?"

"I've... had discussions with them, yes. Although none have been recent."

"Which is how long?" Recker asked.

"In the last six or eight months."

"How easy are these people to find?"

"Not as hard as it should be, to be honest. Knowing you guys, you should have their locations within a day, I would think. They don't advertise or anything, but they're not hard to find."

"I'm sure none of them are going to come out and admit anything. Any tips on getting them to talk?"

Vincent laughed. "You really need tips on getting people to open up?"

"Well, I prefer going the easy route first."

"Just do what you do. That should get them to talk pretty quickly. Threaten them with bodily harm, jail time, or both. That usually does the trick. You have to let them know you mean business. If they think you're just bluffing, they'll try to move on right away."

"I don't do too much bluffing."

"I know. That's why I doubt you'll have too many problems. As long as they know you're not there to blow up their business, I think you'll be fine."

"What about protection?" Haley asked. "Bodyguards?"

"Not that I'm aware of. A couple of them might have a partner or a sidekick or something, but nothing like a group hanging around them or anything."

They continued talking about the list of four names, while also feeding the ducks for a little while. Once they were finished, Recker and Haley stood up to leave. But Haley still had one more question in mind, though not about the current business.

"What was your connection to Chery's father?"

Vincent looked a little puzzled by the question at first. "I see you've done a little digging on your own."

"Just kind of came up in passing."

"So is this a professional question? Or a... personal one?"

"Maybe a little bit of both."

"She does have an attractiveness to her, doesn't she?"

Haley shrugged. "Like I said, just something that came up. But I don't mean to pry if it's not my business."

Vincent lifted his left arm as if he were ambivalent about the situation. "Eh, I suppose there's no harm done. Her father owed me quite a bit of money. Let's just say, he wasn't the greatest at supporting his family. He had his issues. He had his struggles. Too many, to be honest. To make a long story short, he couldn't pay. But instead of doing what many people in my position would do, which is to make an example out of him, I didn't do that. I put him to work for me instead. He paid off his debts that way."

"How's that explain Cheryl?"

"Well, as you know, I don't do business with anybody unless I know everything about them. So I knew he had a family. And I knew they were struggling. He had a kid about to finish high school, wanted to go to college, so I just helped that along."

"Why? Why would it matter?"

"Because when you're in a position to give back, such as I am, I think it's your duty to do so. Sure, I am who I am, I do what I do, but as you well know, I've never engaged with anybody who didn't deserve it, you know what I mean?"

"Yeah."

"This life isn't for everybody. It shouldn't be for everybody. This country needs regular, normal people, doing regular, normal things. That's how it works. And if I can help a young person out, get them on the right path to develop whatever their dreams are, it's something worth doing. She wasn't going to be able to afford school, so I helped her out. As simple as that."

"And you get your hooks into the M.E.'s office?"

Vincent shrugged. "It wasn't as much about that. Sure, I'll use her every once in a while if I have to. But on very rare occasions. And that's not why I did it. She's not a part of this life of ours. Maybe once or twice a year I might need her help with something. That's all. And there's no pressure or anything. And it's nothing that might jeopardize her position or anything."

"I understand," Haley said. "Hope it didn't come across like I was interrogating or anything. Was just curious."

"It's no problem. I can understand wanting some background information on her. Especially if you're considering seeing her outside of... a work environment."

Haley didn't have a reply. He just grinned and

nodded. Recker tapped him on the arm, wanting to get going.

"Well, thanks for the list," Recker said.

Vincent waved at them. "Happy hunting."

"We'll be hunting. But I doubt anyone will be happy about it. Especially the people we talk to."

18

Recker and Haley were waiting for the first name on their list to appear. Recker was leaning up against the side of a parking garage, pretending to be busy on his phone. Haley was on the next street over, doing the exact same thing.

"Hope we don't have to wait out here long," Haley said.

"According to the information, Hyatt is usually around here at this time of day."

"I'm not seeing anyone that looks like him."

"We haven't been here long."

"Yeah, but a couple of guys just hanging out in the same spot for too long is sure to draw some attention."

"We're just waiting to meet up with someone," Recker said. "People do it all the time. Besides, I don't think we'll have to wait very long."

"I sure hope you're right about that."

"I am."

"What makes you so sure?"

"Because I see him right now."

"You do?" Haley asked. "You got him in your sights this very second?"

"I do. He's walking this way."

Recker kept his eyes on him, then looked at his phone so it didn't look like he was waiting for him. Once Hyatt passed Recker's position, he turned right, into the alley between the parking garage and the building next to it.

"Just turned right into the alley," Recker said. After a few moments, Recker moved and followed him. "Be careful. We don't know if he's armed."

Haley turned into the alley from the other end, walking towards them. Not too long after turning in, Hyatt turned his head around, and saw Recker walking in the same direction. Hyatt didn't quite like the look of things. Recker wasn't walking with purpose. He appeared to be a man who was following him, for some reason.

Hyatt turned his head forward again and picked up the pace. He started speed walking, but slowed down again, once he noticed another man in the alley. Both men were walking slowly towards him. He didn't have a good feeling about what was going to happen here. He just stopped, right in the middle of the alley, partially frozen in fear.

"Look, guys, whatever the issue is, we can work it out, right? Right?"

Recker and Haley continued walking towards him, each of them ready to pull his gun if that's how Hyatt wanted to play it. But Hyatt never made a move to indicate he was carrying, so maybe he didn't have one on him. Recker and Haley kept moving closer to Hyatt, making the man backtrack until he was against the wall. There were a few dumpsters next to them, partially concealing them from the street.

Hyatt nervously laughed. "Hey, what's going on guys? Do I know you?"

"We know you," Recker replied.

"Oh. OK. So, uh, what's the deal here?"

"You deal in drugs. And not the most popular ones. We know that."

"I don't know what you're talking about fellas. I really..."

Recker didn't let him finish the lie. He angrily pounded the dumpster with the side of his closed fist. "Don't give me that! Do we really look like the people that you can play with?"

Hyatt licked his lips and took a gulp. He could see he was in serious trouble. "What are you guys? Cops?"

"Do we really look like cops?"

"Well, I mean..."

"Well we're not!"

"Sorry, man, sorry. What do you want out of me?

I'm not doing nothing to nobody. I'm just minding my own business."

Recker chuckled. "Yeah, OK."

"Seriously, who are you guys? I never saw you before."

Recker looked over to his partner and nodded. Haley took out his phone and scrolled to a picture. It was of Addison.

"We're looking for this guy," Haley said.

Hyatt moved his head closer to get a better look. It looked like he was giving it a good look. Then, he shook his head.

"Sorry. Don't think I know the guy."

"He's bought what you specialize in," Recker said.

Hyatt shrugged. "I'm not the only one that sells the junk. He could've gotten it off of anybody."

"From what we understand, you sell the most."

Hyatt smiled. "Well, I'm flattered and all, but I didn't sell nothing to that guy." He could see by the looks on their faces that they didn't believe him. "Trust me, if I knew the guy, I'd say so. You obviously got me backed into a corner, and you don't look like the kind of guys that do well with lies, so I'm just gonna tell you straight up. I ain't seen the guy. Don't know him. I ain't never sold to him, and I don't know his name. So, I'm sorry, but I can't help you."

"Sorry, we don't believe you," Recker said.

Hyatt sighed.

"His name's William Addison," Haley said. "Ring a

bell?"

"Nope. I'm telling you, I don't know that cat."

"How do you get this stuff, anyway?"

A wide smile overtook Hyatt's face. "Well, you know, I got my ways. My sources."

"Tell us about them."

"I can't do that."

Recker put his hand on his waist, making the implication clear. Hyatt wasn't sure if the man was reaching for a gun, but he sure didn't want to find out.

"OK, well, you know, maybe I know a few doctors or whatever, some people in the medical field who may choose to sell a few things on the side. You know, things they don't need anymore, things like that. I can't give you names or anything, though."

Recker pointed to Addison's picture. "And this guy?"

"I keep telling you, I don't know the guy. That's the honest truth, man. I can see you boys mean business. And I'm all about staying healthy, you know? I can see lying to you is probably not a wise business decision. So I ain't gonna do it."

"I hope you're telling us the truth. For your sake. Because if you're not, we know where you live."

"You do?"

"Yeah. We do. And we know where you like to hang out. And we're also pretty tight with Vincent."

"Vincent? Awe, man. What are you guys, like the worst of the worst?"

"Something like that," Recker answered. "So this is your last chance. Because if we find out you're lying to us, there's nowhere you can hide. We will come after you. And we will find you. And nobody's gonna like what they find after we're done with you."

Hyatt took a deep breath, realizing they meant business. "Dude, I get it. You're a couple of badasses. That comes through loud and clear, man. And I'm respecting that. I am. But I'm still being honest with you. I don't know the dude. I ain't never sold to him. Don't know who he is. His name don't ring a bell. Nothing. So, I totally get if I'm lying I'm gonna be a dead man. And I'm cool with that. Well, I mean, not the dying part. But the threat part. I believe it. I do. And that's why I'm confident in saying... this ain't me."

"So if it's not you, who do you think is the next most likely suspect?"

Hyatt shrugged. "If I had to guess, I'd say it's Mekhi. That dude don't care who he sells to or nothing. He'll sell to anybody."

"And you do?" Haley asked.

"Well, I mean, I'm not saying it like that, but... I mean... I try to have some standards, you know?"

"Yeah, I bet."

"Where's the best place to find Mekhi?" Recker asked.

"Shoot, what time is it right now? Probably where he usually is around this time. Probably in bed with some ho he picked up off the street the night before.

That's what he usually does. He's a late riser. Usually don't even get up until noon. I don't even know how the dude operates, to be honest."

"Where can we find him?"

"Permission to go in my pocket for my phone?"

"Go ahead."

Hyatt pulled out his phone and started scrolling through it. He had hundreds of names and addresses in there. He finally got to Mekhi's.

"Yeah, here it is."

Recker took the phone away from him and looked at it. He then took a picture of it with his own phone.

"Yeah, sure, look for yourself," Hyatt said. "It's all cool."

"He better be here."

"You better not warn him we're coming either," Haley said.

Hyatt put his arms up. "No worries, no worries. I don't ever warn nobody that bad news is coming."

"Because if you do, we'll be back to see you."

"I know, I know. And bad things will happen to me. I got that part loud and clear. Believe me, you do your thing and I'll do mine. Hopefully far away from each other."

Recker handed the phone back. "There you go. Thanks for the info."

"Yeah, no prob, man. Glad I could help. Hey, if Mekhi's the guy you're looking for, do I get some kind of finder's fee for helping you out or something?"

Recker and Haley glanced at each other, amazed at the audacity of the man. Hyatt was lucky he was leaving in one piece, and here he wanted to be compensated in some way.

"Yeah, you'll get a finder's fee," Recker said. "You'll get to keep on breathing with all your limbs attached. Does that work for you?"

Hyatt instantly nodded. "Oh, most def, man, yeah. Thank you. That works perfect for me." He cleared his throat a few times. "Um, well, uh, yeah. Yeah. Good luck with that."

"Anything else you'd like to share with us before we go?"

"Can't think of a thing, man. Except, uh, yeah, good luck. Good luck."

Recker faked a smile. "Thanks. Remember...?"

"You'll be back, I know, I know. Trust me, I don't ever wanna see you guys again. Go do your thing and all."

Recker and Haley walked away and slipped out of the alley. Back on the street, they looked at the address for Mekhi.

"How far away?" Haley asked.

"Twenty minutes or so. Not too bad. We should be there before the guy wakes up."

"Guess he's gonna be in for a surprise, huh?"

"It's not gonna be sweet dreams for him, that's for sure. Let's make him wake up right into a nightmare."

19

Recker and Haley were outside Mekhi's door, listening to what was going on inside. There was nothing but silence. They figured he was still probably sleeping. Then Haley got to work in trying to pick the lock. Recker stood watch.

Within a minute, Haley got it. But the door still wasn't opening.

"Must be a deadbolt or something," Haley said.

"That complicates things."

Haley pulled on the door a couple times. "Doesn't feel like one of the best I've ever felt. Might be able to bust through it."

"And make a lot of noise in the process."

"I can still try to pick the deadbolt."

"Let's try to think of another way," Recker said.

"What about the balcony? I saw one on the way in."

"Second floor."

"We can climb up to it."

Recker thought about it for a moment, then agreed. They left the inside of the apartments and went back outside. Once they located the right balcony, they started climbing. They got on top of the railing of a first floor unit, then jumped up and grabbed hold of the bottom of the railing on the second floor. They each pulled themselves up, crawling over it on the second floor.

Now on the balcony of Mekhi's apartment, they pulled on the sliding glass door that led inside. It slid right open.

"Guess he's not too security conscious," Haley said.

"More like he doesn't expect strangers to come in this way."

They stepped inside and immediately started looking around. The place was a mess. Clothes, food, and trash was all over the place.

"This is a pigsty," Haley said. "How does this guy operate like this?"

Recker didn't have an answer. They proceeded to the bedroom, where they assumed Mekhi was. The door was halfway open. Recker pushed the door open all the way, seeing two bodies lying on the bed, the sheets pulled up over their heads.

Recker went over to the bed, taking his gun out. He quickly pulled the sheets down. As soon as the bodies moved, Recker pointed his gun at Mekhi's head. The woman, upon seeing the gun, immediately jumped up and got out of bed, screaming. She didn't even care that she had no clothes on. She was only interested in staying alive.

"Please don't kill me! Please don't kill me! I didn't do anything! I promise!"

Recker didn't pay much attention to her screaming, though. He was focused squarely on Mekhi and making sure he didn't make any sudden movements. Haley was the one dealing with the woman. He put his finger in the air to hopefully quiet her down.

"Stop that," Haley said in a calm voice. She didn't listen at first. Now he said it in a more firm voice. "Stop that. Now."

The woman instantly quieted down, though she still looked fearful. She put her hands up.

"Put them down. I can see you're not, um… packing."

"I didn't do anything," she said.

"Calm down, put your clothes on, and get out of here."

"What? Really?"

"Yeah. But hurry it up. We don't have all day."

The woman quickly scoured around the floor, looking for her clothes. She found a shirt that wasn't hers, but she didn't care very much at the moment. She hurried and put it on, then found some pants. She didn't bother with any undergarments. She didn't even care about her shoes. She took a look around for them, but since she didn't see them initially, she just left them behind.

"Um, can I go?"

"You don't want shoes?" Haley asked.

"Not really. I'm good."

Haley shrugged. "Take off, if you want."

"Call me later, babe. If you get out of here."

The woman shot out of the bedroom like she was a short-distance runner trying to make her best time in the forty.

"I'll call you!" Mekhi shouted.

Haley casually walked out of the bedroom after her, making sure she left the apartment. The door was swinging wide open by the time Haley got there. He closed and locked it, then proceeded back into the bedroom, where his partner still had a gun pointed at Mekhi's face.

"Hey, hey, gents, what's this all about?" Mekhi asked, trying to sound happy and upbeat, though he was terrified inside.

"This is about you, drugs, and a guy named William Addison," Recker replied. "Anything ring a bell? And I'd think long and hard about answering in a non-truthful manner."

Mekhi gulped as he looked at the man with the gun. He certainly didn't look like someone who wanted to play games.

"So, uh, what is it that you wanna know?"

"I already told you," Recker answered.

"So what's in it for me if I tell you?"

"I'll tell you what's gonna be in you if you don't. Lead."

"You know, it sure would be nice if I didn't have that gun pointed at my face."

"I'm sure it would. But it's not moving."

Mekhi gulped again. "It's, uh, making me a little nervous."

"It's supposed to. Now, this is gonna go one of two ways. You can start talking about what we wanna know, or I'm gonna start putting some holes in you one by one until you do. I'll start with your feet and work my way up."

"Hey, man, there's no need for all that violence. Just be cool."

"You supplied drugs to William Addison?"

"The name doesn't really sound familiar."

Recker didn't look pleased. He instantly lowered his weapon to the man's leg.

"No, no, don't! I mean, maybe I know the guy, but I don't recognize the name! Maybe he gave me something else, I don't know!"

Recker glanced at his partner, who took out his phone to bring up Addison's picture. He brought it over to the bed and held it out for Mekhi to look at.

"Look familiar?" Haley asked.

"Uh, yeah, yeah, maybe."

"This isn't really a maybe question," Recker said. "You either know him or you don't."

"I don't think..." Mekhi said.

Recker didn't like where that statement was headed, and pressed his gun on Mekhi's thigh.

"Wounds like this are usually messy. And sometimes fatal in this spot. Along with a massive amount of pain. You ever been shot before? It's not pleasant. Some people pass out from the pain."

"Yeah, really doesn't sound enticing," Mekhi said. "I'd rather not do it."

"Then answer our questions, and then we'll be out of here. And you won't need a trip to the emergency room."

"How do I know you won't just shoot me anyway?"

"Well, I could shoot you either way. But one way, you're definitely getting shot. The other way, maybe you'll actually live through this. So really, the best thing you can do is take your chances and tell us what we want to know."

Mekhi sighed, but knew he was up the creek either way. But Recker was right. If he lied, he thought he was definitely getting shot. The other way, maybe he had a chance. He wasn't certain of that. But he was certain what would happen if he didn't say what these guys wanted to know.

"Guess I don't have much of a choice here, do I?"

"Not much," Recker replied. "I mean, you do have the choice of being an idiot if you want. But I wouldn't recommend it."

Haley continued holding his phone up. "You know this guy or not?"

Mekhi took another look at the picture, not that he really needed to. "Yeah. Yeah, I know him. I don't know him as... whatever you said his name was, though."

"William Addison."

"Yeah. I don't know about all that."

"What name do you know him by?"

"Honestly? Can't remember." He saw by the looks on the faces of Recker and Haley that they didn't believe him. "I'm not even lying. He told me his name and that was it. I didn't really care. It was Joe, or Steve, or Tom, or... I don't even know what. It's one of those things that you hear and then forget real quick, you know?"

"When did you do business with him?" Recker asked.

"I don't know. A month? Six weeks? Something like that. I don't exactly keep records of my transactions."

"How many times?"

"Just the one. That was it. Never seen him before or since."

"How'd you get in touch with him to begin with?"

"How's anybody get in touch with me? He contacted me. We talked. I felt him out like I do with everybody to make sure he was legit. Then we did business."

"You have his phone number?"

"Nope."

"Then how'd you talk?" Recker asked.

"By phone. But I delete everything in my phone every three days, man. Can't trust many people these days. Just in case I'm ever raided or something by the police, I like to keep my phone clear."

"You know they can still check your phone records, right?"

"What? How?"

Recker shook his head. "Never mind. So do you have any ideas on where we can find this guy?"

"Haven't a clue. Like I said, haven't heard from him since we did our business."

"Where was that?"

"I don't know. An alley somewhere. Dark, middle of the night, no people around."

"How many pills did you sell him? It was pills, right?"

"Yeah, it was pills. It was... six, I think. Yeah, six."

"Six? You're sure?"

Mekhi nodded. "Yeah, pretty sure."

"He tell you what he was doing with him?"

"Nah. I don't ask, and they don't say. You know how it goes. You don't pry into another man's business."

"Good life advice," Recker said. "Except that man's killed four people with the drugs that you supplied. So I'm no legal expert, but I'm pretty sure that makes you an accessory."

"Wait, what? No. No."

"Oh yeah. He's killed four people."

A worried look suddenly overtook Mekhi's face. "No. No. I didn't know. If I knew he was planning on killing people with it, I wouldn't have sold it to him."

"It's a drug that sedates people. What exactly did you think he was doing with it?"

"I don't know. I thought it was one of these weird new kicks people get on these days. You know, they mix things, try different stuff, all different crap. I thought he was only using it for himself or friends or something. I mean, that's what everyone does, isn't it?"

"Apparently not."

"Oh, man."

"So I'm gonna ask you again. Do you know where this guy is?"

"I don't, man. I really don't. If I did, I'd tell you. I swear I would."

"About how long was it that he contacted you before you met him?" Recker asked.

"It was about a week or so. Somewhere around there. Hey, you guys ain't cops, right? Since you broke in here, I'm assuming you're not. So who are you?"

"Doesn't matter to you. But if I were you, I'd stop doing what you're doing."

"And do what? Work a regular nine-to-five at some fast-food joint or something?"

"Well, if you were, you wouldn't be dealing with killers and facing jail time, would you?"

"I ain't going to jail, man. I'll be getting out of here. Like, tonight. Assuming you let me leave."

"Anything else you can tell us about this guy?" Recker asked.

"Not really. Our conversations were short. And when we made the deal, we barely talked at all."

"He pay in cash?"

"Yeah, man, I don't do Venmo or anything. Too many ways to track that stuff."

After talking with Mekhi a little while longer, Recker and Haley figured they had gotten everything they were going to. The man didn't seem to know a lot, other than the basics. But if they talked on the phone, Jones might be able to track the number down that way. It was more than what they had.

Recker put his gun back in its holster. "Thanks for the information. We'll be going now."

Mekhi breathed a sigh of relief, thankful that he appeared to be escaping the day with his life intact. Recker and Haley then left the room and walked out of the apartment. They talked about what they learned as they went back to their car.

"You sure it's a good idea to just leave this guy?" Haley asked.

Recker shrugged. "What else are we gonna do with him? Taking him out isn't exactly going to solve anything. We still won't know where Addison is, and whoever goes to him for drugs will just go to someone else."

"Could gift wrap him to the cops."

"I dunno. Maybe. My focus right now is finding the

worst of the two evils. And one thing's for sure, this guy bought six pills. That means he's still got two left."

"And two more victims."

"Assuming he hasn't used them yet. That means we've gotta find him fast. Before he can put two more in the ground."

"I'll call David," Haley said. "See if he can tap into Mekhi's phone records."

"Hopefully that'll be the link that we need. God knows we need a break somewhere. Let's hope this is it."

20

By the time Recker and Haley walked through the office door, Jones was waiting for them. He swiveled his chair around, giving off the vibe that he had something to say. Recker and Haley stopped dead in their tracks.

"You got something?" Recker asked.

Jones nodded. "I do. I have a name to go with the face of our friend at the fast food place."

Recker made a face. That wasn't the one that he wanted. He was hoping Jones had already got into Mekhi's phone records and picked out Addison. Jones could see the disappointment on his friend's face.

"I can let it go if you want."

"No," Recker said. "I was just hoping it'd be Addison."

"I've just barely got into phone records. That will take a little more time."

"Figured as much."

"But, as I mentioned, I do have the name of the other guy."

"What's his story?" Haley asked.

"Low-level criminal," Jones replied.

"I'd say he's stepped up to the big time," Recker said. "Him and his friends killed five people."

"Up until this point, low-level. Anyway, I've got him and his three friends."

"You got all of them?"

"Well, I wish I could say it was because of my elite detective skills, but I won't. Once I got the main guy, he basically broadcasted it all over his social media pages."

"Really? How so?"

"This was one of his posts." Jones grabbed a piece of paper where he'd written everything down and started reading from it. "'Going out with my boys tonight. Gonna grab us a bigger piece of the pie. We're gonna make a splash and watch some people die'."

"Wow," Haley said. "He really did broadcast it, didn't he?"

"It gets better. He even tagged three other people in his post, who I'd assume would be the other three with him."

"What do they say?" Recker said. "Stupid don't fall far from the tree."

"Nice rhyme, though," Haley replied.

"What do you have on this foursome?"

"Gangsters. Would-be gangsters. However you like to call it. Going through their social media feeds, all of them, it appears this was nothing more than them trying to make a statement about their arrival in the game."

"Taking over territory?"

"That would be my guess, yes."

"So nothing to do with Addison?" Recker asked.

"If there is, I can't find anything to substantiate it. It appears to be completely non-related."

"How's Jamar connected, though?" Haley asked.

"None of these guys have a tie to Addison?" Recker said.

"Not that I can find," Jones replied.

"What about possible targets for Addison? He's supposedly still got two pills left."

"I'm still working on that too. I've got a lot of balls in the air here."

"None of them seem to be landing."

"Not true," Jones said. "I've identified the men that took out T-Bone's crew."

"He's not our main priority, though."

"It's something to work on until we've got something more concrete with Addison. That's the best I can do right now. I'll continue going over Mekhi's phone records. I'll see if I can locate Addison through that. And I'll keep on looking for possible targets."

"Seems like that leaves these other four to us," Haley said.

Recker nodded. "Yeah."

Seconds later, one of Recker's alternate phones in the desk drawer rang. He eagerly reached in to pick it up. It was T-Bone.

"Hey, you want in on this?"

"In on what?" Recker asked.

"These boys that done shot up my crew, that's what."

"I'm ready to drop some thunder on these bums. I know who they are. I know where they are. And I'm about to get some payback. You want in?"

"I'm not in this for payback. They didn't kill anyone I know."

"Just the same, man. You were there. They shot at you too, you know. Just thought maybe you'd want in the game."

"You got other people with you?" Recker asked.

"Yeah, I got a few peeps. The more the merrier, though, right? If you and the other guy want in, I'll save you a spot. We're about to take care of this now, though."

"We just found out the names of the guys too."

"Nice. But that don't matter now."

"I wouldn't charge into anything if I were you. Just wait them out."

"Nah. Can't do that. They started this. I'm gonna finish it. They ain't getting off the hook that easy."

"No one said anything about getting off the hook. All I'm saying is don't charge in there, wherever you're going, and make a mistake that you won't recover from."

"It's all good, man. I ain't making no mistake. We're taking these bums out!"

"And where is this taking place?"

"Couple blocks away. Don't worry. You'll be hearing about this on the news. I got someone to lure them in. Gonna pick them off like fishes in a pond, you know?"

"All right, tell me where this is happening?" Recker said. "Maybe we can get down there at some point." After T-Bone told him of where the ambush was supposedly going to take place, Recker still tried to talk him down a little. "I still think you should wait. Take your time. These guys aren't going anywhere."

"I know that, man. They been shouting about this all over social media. Talking a big game, talking about how they're gonna be the big dogs and all that. But we're gonna drop them right now. Show them I ain't someone they wanna mess with."

Recker continued trying to talk to him for the next few minutes. He didn't seem to be getting through to him, though. As he kept trying, Haley's phone rang. It was Cheryl.

"Hey, hope I'm not disturbing anything important?"

"Well, just... different things going on," Haley answered.

"Sounds like you're busy. I'll try to keep this brief,

then. I wasn't sure if you wanted to come down here to look at something."

"Look at what?"

"Another body. One came in this morning. Drowning victim. Pulled from the river. No visible marks or injuries."

"Just like the others."

"Just like the others," she said. "Thought you guys might wanna take a look."

"Thanks. I'm not sure yet when we'll be able to get down there."

"No problem. Just figured I'd let you know."

"Thanks. Um, about last night..."

"It's fine. Really. I'm not upset or mad or anything."

"No, I don't want you to think I canceled because I wasn't interested or backing out or anything. We just got really busy with things."

"It's OK. Really. I get it. Like I said, I wasn't mad."

"I'm still interested in having that pizza with you," Haley said. "If you're still interested."

There was a brief hesitation. "Yeah. I am."

"Sounds like today might not be the day for it, though. How available are you in the next few days if I call at the last minute?"

"I'm always available."

As soon as they finished up their conversation, Haley put the phone back in his pocket. He looked at Recker, who had ended his talk a minute earlier.

"You wanna head down to this... conflict?" Recker asked.

Haley put his hand up. "Might wanna pump the brakes on that."

"Why?"

"We got another body."

"What? Where?"

"Cheryl just called. A body came in this morning. Same as the others. Pulled from the river. No marks."

"Any ID?"

"Not yet," Haley replied.

Recker sighed. "Pretty soon we won't need to identify any other targets for Addison. He'll have taken them all out already."

"To be fair, seems like we got dragged into this pretty late in the game. We're just playing catchup right now."

"So what's your plan?" Jones asked.

"I say we go check this body out," Haley answered. "Whatever fight T-Bone's walking into, that's his deal. If he takes those guys out, all the better for us. Means we won't have to deal with them."

"And if T-Bone loses?" Recker asked.

"Then it'll be our turn. But from the sounds of it, I'm not sure we'd get there in time to help him anyway."

Recker scratched his forehead. "Yeah, he wasn't too interested in waiting. His mind's already made up about what he's doing."

"Check this body out, then?"

Recker nodded. "Yeah. Maybe we'll get lucky with it." He started to walk away, then something occurred to him. "Hey, wasn't last night your date with Cheryl? How'd it go?"

"Uh, it didn't. I canceled."

"What? Why?"

"Yeah, we were into it pretty good with everything, so..."

"I'm sorry. Maybe you'll be able to reschedule."

"Yeah, I think we'll figure something out."

"Good. Don't put it on the back burner, though. Figure out a time. I know we're busy, but... you know."

"We will. It's something that... I want to."

Recker tapped him on the arm. "Good. Let's go see this body. And her."

Haley smiled. "Guess that's the only good thing about going down there."

"Oh, dear, we're doing this again," Jones said.

"Stop," Recker said. "It's not the same. And we're not getting into it again."

"Agreed. Agreed."

"Anyway, let's check this body out. While we're doing that, maybe T-Bone will take care of business for us. That'll mean one less thing on our plate. And right now, we could use it."

"Not for nothing, but do you think we might have a T-Bone problem too?"

"What do you mean?"

"We know he's selling drugs. Sometimes to teenagers. Are we just going to pretend like he's our friend, even after he takes out these other guys?"

Recker stared straight ahead for a second. "No. But right now, he's not our enemy. Let's focus on finding Addison first. Then after that... all bets are off."

21

As Recker and Haley pulled onto Callowhill Street, they saw Cheryl standing outside, leaning against the side of the building. She had a folder in her hands that she was reading. They parked their car, then walked over to her. As they approached, she closed the folder.

She smiled at them, particularly Haley. "Hi."

"Nice to see you," Haley replied.

"You too."

Recker didn't want to interrupt their introductions, but they really did have business to discuss. "Thanks for calling about the body."

"Oh. Yeah. Follow me."

They followed Cheryl inside, not stopping until they got to the room with the body lying in the middle of it on a slab. The sheet was pulled up over the head, just like the last time. She walked over to it and gently pulled the sheet down to the middle of the waist.

"Not much different than the others," she said.

Recker and Haley walked over to the dead man, casually inspecting it. They didn't bother with a thorough examination, as they knew Cheryl had already done that.

"No marks at all," Recker said.

"No, but since I called, I may have gotten some additional info for you."

"Like what?"

Cheryl went over to her desk, a smile on her face. "Oh, like, I dunno... a name?"

Recker and Haley's eyes lit up.

"A name?" Recker said.

"How'd you get that?" Haley asked.

"Oh, I have my ways," she answered. "I may not be a big detective like you guys, but I got a few tricks up my sleeve."

She picked up a folder and put it down, opening it, while also turning it around for the others to see. Recker and Haley walked over to it to look at it.

"You wanna leave the room?" Recker asked.

Cheryl waved him off. "What's the point?"

They read the chart, and Recker's eyes immediately went to the name. He read it a couple of times.

"Why does that name sound familiar?"

"We've seen it before," Haley replied.

"But where?"

They both looked at it for a few more seconds. Finally, Haley snapped his fingers.

"Some of the names that David pulled up. People in Addison's background."

Recker nodded, remembering, though he didn't recall exactly what this person did. "Yeah. Yeah, I remember now. This guy gave music lessons, didn't he?"

"Yeah. To some of the adopted kids. Not just Frank's, but a bunch of others too."

"This guy's taking out everyone in his past."

"Not everyone," Haley said. "There's more than six. But he's only got pills for six."

"And used five."

"But what makes these six so special that he's targeting them?"

"Either he feels like they wronged him the most, or he just has a special hatred for them."

"But who's the last one gonna be?"

"We're assuming he's only got six targets," Recker said. "Who's to say he doesn't have more? Maybe he's got more pills. Or he's using a different method for the others."

"It's gonna be hard finding him by trying to find his next target. I'm sure he interacted with hundreds of people in the foster care system, not to mention after Frank took him."

"We're gonna have to hope that David can find something in Mekhi's records that can lead us to him."

"Who's David?" Cheryl asked.

Recker cleared his throat. "Oh, um, just a... just a guy."

"How many people do you have in this operation of yours?"

"Feels like not enough."

"You're very secretive."

"I have to be."

"Fair enough," she said.

"The only thing we do know is he's got access to a swimming pool," Haley mentioned. "But is it one at his house? At an apartment complex? Some community pool?"

"Or is he house-sitting?" Recker added.

"We can't check every house with a swimming pool."

"We could check out apartment complexes that might have one."

"I feel like he wouldn't use one of those, though. Too many eyes might be on him. Five bodies so far, you figure somebody would see him by now. Even by accident."

"Yeah, probably so. Community pool?"

"Yeah, maybe," Haley said. "But it'd probably have to be at night or outside of operating hours. He'd need to be alone."

"You guys ever consider him being a lawn caretaker or something?" Cheryl asked. "Or maybe he's a pool contractor. If he's taking care of someone's pool while they're on vacation, he'd obviously know they weren't there."

Recker and Haley looked at each other. They thought she might have stumbled on something.

"There's an idea," Haley said. "And it makes a ton of sense."

Cheryl smiled and turned her head as if she were embarrassed. She was happy to contribute something, even if she still didn't know them all that well.

"It was just an idea."

"And it's a good one," Haley replied.

"David can't find him through any records," Recker said. "Which means whatever he's doing, he's not on someone's payroll. Probably getting paid in cash."

"If he's on some lawn crew or something, that could fit."

"Still gonna be a problem finding him, even if that's true. Those guys don't advertise their employees, especially if they're illegal or have some criminal trail behind them. So he could work anonymously, without anyone knowing anything about him."

"Other than whoever hired him."

"And he might not care other than that he shows up."

"And you know all those outfits don't keep computer records," Haley said. "So David won't be able to hack into it and find out."

"There's no way to tell who they're servicing that might be on vacation. And that's assuming we're even on the right track." Recker slapped his leg in frustration. "Just feels like we're swimming around in circles."

Cheryl chuckled. "That's funny. Swimming around. Cause we're talking about swimming pools. That's, um..." She realized no one was laughing with her. "Uh, yeah, no, not really funny. Just ignore that."

"Well, at least we got something else to look into," Haley said.

"Feels like that's all we get. And keep getting. We keep getting possibilities, but it doesn't feel like we're actually any closer to this guy than when we started."

"He's pretty smart. Living off-grid. Probably making some good money since those pills aren't cheap. Getting paid in cash. Paying rent, bills, groceries in cash. Probably has a prepaid phone. No social media presence. Doing it the right way if you don't wanna be found."

"Yeah, he sure is. Be nice if he tripped up somewhere along the line, though."

"I'm sure somebody must know him," Cheryl said. "I'm sure he's not a hermit, right?"

Recker looked at his partner. "Maybe we can have David check all the security and traffic cameras for the past couple of months. Plug his picture in, see if we get any hits."

"Who's this David guy again?"

Recker ignored her. "If we get enough in one area, we can start narrowing it down."

"Who's David?"

"Good idea," Haley said.

"He's able to check cameras? What's he do?"

Neither one of them was going to confirm Jones or what he did for them. They just kept ignoring the question.

"You guys are like at CIA-level in dodging questions. Did you ever work for them or something?"

Both Recker and Haley just gave her a glance. She clapped her hands together and smiled.

"Oh my God, you did, didn't you?"

Haley put his finger against his lips. "Shh. They might be listening."

Cheryl immediately started looking around. "What? Really?"

Haley smiled. "No. I'm just kidding."

"Oh my gosh." She put her hand over her chest. "You almost gave me a heart attack."

"Let's head back to the office and start running things," Recker said.

"What about T-Bone?" Haley asked.

Recker snapped his fingers, forgetting about that situation. "Right. Let's swing by there, see if we can move things along there."

"Who's T-Bone?" Cheryl asked. "Does he work for you too?"

"No, T-Bone's a gangster," Haley answered.

"Is he involved in this? I'm so confused."

"So are we," Recker replied. "Let's head over there and see what's going on."

Haley glanced at Cheryl. "Maybe call you later?"

"I'll have my phone nearby. I'm still craving that pizza."

As they were saying their goodbyes, Recker tried calling T-Bone. He didn't pick up, though. Recker tried a couple more times. He still got no response.

"He's not picking up," Recker said.

"Could be knee-deep in it."

"Could be."

"Or it might mean a lot of things," Haley said.

"Could. But none of them are good."

22

Recker and Haley rolled up on the address that T-Bone gave them. It was an alley behind a used appliance store that was no longer in business. They didn't see any cars in the vicinity. And it seemed quiet. Not that that was always a good thing.

They approached the area cautiously. Their guns weren't out yet, but they were ready to withdraw them at a moment's notice should the need arise for them. They started walking through the alley, keeping their eyes open. They were listening for even the slightest of sounds.

After they walked through the entire alley, without a hint of any type of conflict, they stopped at the end of it.

"This is it, right?" Haley asked.

Recker pulled out his phone and checked what he wrote down. "Yeah. This is what he told me."

"Maybe it was a false alarm. Maybe the intel he got was wrong and nothing happened."

"Could be. But why didn't he answer the phone?"

Haley shrugged. "Could've gotten busy. Try him again."

Recker dialed T-Bone's number, but he didn't get any different of a result than the previous time. He shook his head as the phone kept ringing.

"Nothing."

There were two doors in the back of the building. Haley thought he detected one of them move slightly as a gust of wind came through.

Haley pointed to the building with his thumb. "You don't suppose they're in there, do you?"

"Anything's possible, I suppose."

"I thought I detected that one door move a little as the wind blew."

"Might as well check it out while we're here."

They went over to the door closest to them. They took their guns out as they stood next to it. Haley put his hand on the knob. He pulled it right open. They looked at each other.

Recker, as he prepared to go in, brought his weapon up to his chest. Once he went in, it was a little tough to see at first, but there was some natural light coming in through a few windows at the front of the building that weren't boarded up yet. Haley followed his partner inside.

Not knowing what they were walking into, if

anything, they stuck close together. They didn't want to split up and run into trouble without the support of the other one. It was clear soon enough that none of that would be necessary, though.

It only took a few minutes to figure out what was going on there. They came across the first body lying on the floor, face down, several bullet holes in his back. Recker knelt down next to the man and checked for a pulse. The bullet holes and blood told the story, but he wanted to make sure there wasn't an ounce of breath left in him. There wasn't.

"He's gone."

Haley was about to reply, but then he saw another large lump in the middle of the room. He tapped his partner on the arm and pointed to it.

"Looks like we got another one over there."

They both went in that direction, both keeping their guns out and pointed in case trouble was still lurking. Once they reached the body, he was just like the other one. Face down on the floor, multiple bullet holes in his back.

"Nothing left of him, either," Recker said.

"Don't recognize either of them. Wonder who they belong to?"

They kept walking around the room, finding a third body not long after. This one was on his back, though. But the result was the same. And he had multiple bullet holes, like the others. There wasn't a breath left within him.

"Who are these guys?" Haley asked.

Recker had his suspicions, but he wasn't going to voice them until they had proof. But he had a feeling they'd find that proof soon enough. And they did. They kept walking throughout the room, finding a fourth victim. This was one they recognized.

The body was lying on its side, his arm stretched out, the man's face on his arm for support. Recker knelt down and pushed the body onto its back. It was T-Bone.

"Looks like we found out why he didn't answer," Haley said.

This was what Recker suspected he'd find. He looked at T-Bone's chest, which was soaked with blood. He didn't feel sad or any remorse over the man's death. He knew what T-Bone was. But he didn't feel happy about it either. It was just how things went in this line of business.

"I'd say T-Bone didn't quite get what he bargained for."

"Well, I did tell him to slow down and not rush into things," Recker replied.

"Fatal mistake."

"These guys always feel like they're too tough to listen."

They kept on going throughout the room, making sure there were no other bodies. There were, though. They found two more. After they'd gone through everything, they took pictures of all their faces, so

Jones could run them through the computer. They suspected that they were all parts of T-Bone's crew, but there was always a chance one of them wasn't. And if one of them wasn't, that could help provide a lead towards the others.

"What do you think went down here?" Haley asked.

Recker shrugged. "Tough to say. They're all spread out, so I'd say they weren't jumped immediately. Either that, or they all scattered as soon as the bullets started flying. But I guess anything's possible."

They continued looking around the room, hoping to find some clue, or evidence that was left behind. They didn't notice anything obvious, though. They did go through each of the dead man's pockets, removing anything of note. The only thing any of them had on them was their phone. And that was only two of them. Either the rest didn't have one on them, or they got taken after they were killed.

"Guess that pretty much wraps things up here," Haley said.

Recker sighed. "Yeah, I guess it does. Really wish this would've turned out differently. I feel like if T-Bone had come out of this on top, we wouldn't have had to deal with him right away. We'd have some time. But these other guys..."

"They're becoming a problem."

"A big problem. And one we've got to deal with now before it gets even bigger."

"How do you wanna deal with them?"

"First, we've gotta find them," Recker answered. "Once we do that, we'll beat them at their own game."

"I don't think they're too big yet. Handful of guys. That'll help us."

"It should. But one thing's for sure. We're gonna be seeing them soon. And we'll be bringing the lead. Next time, they're the ones who are gonna be lying on the ground with more bullet holes than you can count."

"First we gotta find them."

Recker nodded. "That we do. But we will. One way or another... we will."

23

Recker and Haley were walking down the alley in order to get back to their car. Recker's phone rang, and he saw that it was Jones calling. He picked it up, ready to tell him about their findings with T-Bone's men. But he never got the chance. Jones immediately started rambling.

"OK, you need to get over to 2215 West Sycamore right now."

"What?" Recker said. "Why the urgency?"

"I believe that is where you will find Mr. Addison."

"What? How do you know?"

"No time for that. Just trust me. I believe that is where he is living at the moment. Head over there."

Recker and Haley instantly picked up the pace and jogged back to their car. As they got on the road, Recker still had more questions about what they were walking into.

"This a house or an apartment?"

"It appears to be an apartment," Jones answered.

"Do they have a swimming pool?"

"Not that I can tell. That is a question for another time, though. All that matters is that I believe Addison is there. We can find out the particulars later."

As they drove and put the address into their GPS, they saw they were still close to thirty minutes away.

"Address doesn't strike me as familiar," Haley said.

"No, I don't think we've been to this one before," Recker replied. "David, do you believe he is there at this exact minute?"

"That I cannot be sure of," Jones answered. "I do think this is his current residence, however."

"Can you tell me how you figure that?"

"I have done some deductions and determined this is the result. The how's and the why's don't really matter right now, do they?"

"No, I suppose not."

"And you two should be getting ready."

"Yeah," Recker said. "What's his number?"

"336. I believe that to be the third floor."

"All right. Thanks. Call you when we're done."

"Good luck."

With Haley driving, Recker started looking the address up on his phone, wanting to get more familiar with the surroundings of the apartment. It didn't look like anything out of the ordinary, though. Just a basic apartment building, with one entrance that led to several hallways with the specific units. Only units on the ground floor had the opportunity to enter elsewhere through the back patio.

"This kind of came out of nowhere," Haley said.

"That's how it goes sometimes."

"Wonder how David ran him down."

"I dunno. Maybe he got a hit off the phone number from Mekhi's phone. He's right, though. Doesn't really matter right now. Now we just need to focus on what we're doing once we get there."

"Well, third floor. Doesn't sound like he's got anywhere to go. One way in, one way out."

Recker didn't seem so sure. "Feels like kind of a weird spot for him. You'd think you'd pick a spot with more escape paths in case you're discovered."

"Maybe he really didn't think about it like that. Or maybe he doesn't think he's ever getting caught."

"Always possible, I guess."

Recker continued looking at the map of the apartment building, eventually finding something that worried him.

"That might be a problem."

"What's that?" Haley asked.

"Fire escape."

"There goes the one way in and out."

"I think maybe we should split up here," Recker said. "One of us takes the door, the other waits outside by the fire escape ladder. That way if he ducks out, we're still waiting for him."

"Sounds like the only plan we got."

"Assuming he's there to begin with."

Though they continued talking about it and formulating a plan, they did agree to split up like they discussed. It was the only way to be sure they had all the angles covered. Once they reached the apartment building and parked, they waited in the car for a little while. Like most buildings, they saw a few people coming and going, and walking outside. But none of them were Addison. Not that they really expected him to just walk into their view, but it would have been nice to be thrown a bone.

After sitting and waiting for about twenty minutes, they decided to take matters into their own hands. They got out of the car and walked over to the building. Recker went inside, while Haley went to the back of the building to cover the fire escape.

Once Recker got to the third floor, he immediately found unit 336. He put his ear up to the door before doing anything. He thought he detected some voices. It could have been the TV. It wasn't very loud, but he could hear a couple different voices. He touched his ear to communicate with his partner.

"I'm hearing something inside," Recker said.

"I'm in position, so... whenever you're ready."

Recker turned his head in both directions, just to make sure no one else was coming. He wasn't busting through the door. Well, not yet at least. He was going to try it the old-fashioned way first. Knock. But if the door opened, and the bullets started flying quickly, he didn't want there to be anyone walking in the hallways that could wind up a casualty.

The coast was clear. So Recker put his fist on the door and knocked three times. He continued listening inside. The TV suddenly turned off, or the volume was lowered, as he couldn't hear it at all now. There was no doubt somebody was in there.

Nobody came to the door to answer, though. But Recker wasn't giving up. He knocked again. The door still never opened. Now Recker had to decide whether he was going to continue knocking and be a pest until whoever was in there had enough of it and decided to open, or whether he'd just try to knock it down.

It didn't have to be an either/or proposition, though. He could do both. He continued knocking, wanting to exhaust that possibility first.

"Hey, what's going on up there? You in yet?"

Recker touched his ear. "Not yet. Still knocking, waiting for a response."

"Sounds like you're not getting one."

"Well I'm gonna..."

Recker didn't finish his thought, as he thought he detected footsteps getting louder, and closer. Then, he heard what sounded like the door being unlocked. Then, it opened. Just a crack. A portion of a man's face appeared. But it was enough for Recker to get a positive confirmation. It was William Addison.

"Help you?"

"William Addison?" Recker asked.

The man shook his head. "Nobody here by that name. You got the wrong apartment."

"I don't think I do. I wanna talk to you."

Addison sighed. "All right. Let me just open the door up fully."

He quickly closed the door, but Recker anticipated the move. Recker crashed into the door, breaking it open before Addison had a chance to lock it again. Recker stumbled as he went through the door, getting down on one knee to regain his balance. Just as he was about to get up, a box came flying at him to knock him down to the ground fully. Recker glanced up, seeing Addison just as he made his way out the window.

"Chris, coming your way!"

"I see him," Haley said, looking up, and seeing Addison climb out the window.

Haley didn't see the need to make a move yet. Addison had to come down to him. He tried to stay out of sight so he didn't spook Addison before he got there. It didn't quite work how Haley hoped it would, though. Addison looked down before he started descending, and saw Haley standing there. He got the vibe that Haley was waiting for him. Even if he wasn't, Addison wasn't taking any chances. He went the other direction instead.

"Mike, he's going up."

Recker then appeared in the window and climbed through it. He took a quick look down at Haley, then looked up and saw Addison ascending.

"I got him," Recker said, also starting to climb up. "You try to figure out where he's going and meet him wherever he comes down."

"That could be anywhere."

"Gotta be a way down somewhere. Just try to find it."

"I'm on it."

Addison had a little bit of a head start on his pursuer, but Recker thought he could still catch him. He didn't know where they were going, but there was always the possibility that Addison didn't know either. Recker assumed they were heading to the roof. He was thrown for a surprise when Addison suddenly stopped and launched himself through an opened window on the sixth floor.

"He just went inside another apartment," Recker said, trying to keep his partner updated on the pursuit.

Recker could already hear the screams of a woman as he got to the sixth floor balcony. He went inside, immediately seeing a middle-aged woman standing there, a worried look on her face as she saw him.

"Which way did he go?" Recker asked.

"He went out the door!" she yelled. "Get him!"

Recker ran towards the front door, which was partially open. He stopped in the hallway, looking to both sides. He didn't see Addison at first. Then he looked at the end of the hallway to his right, seeing a door slowly close. Recker ran in that direction. It was the stairs that led down to the first floor.

Recker pushed the door open quickly and rushed down the steps. He didn't have Addison in sight yet, but he knew he had to be close. Recker still didn't have eyes on him as he reached the bottom floor. Once he got there, Recker pushed the door open, and was about to run full steam ahead. But he stopped abruptly before he had a chance to get started. Haley was standing right in front of him.

"Hey, where'd he go?" Recker asked.

Haley stuck his arms out to both sides. "Didn't come this way."

"He had to. I followed him down this way."

"I've been standing here for a couple minutes figuring he'd come down this way. Haven't seen him."

Recker puffed and put his hands on his hips as he turned completely around to figure out their next steps.

"Where'd he go?" Recker asked.

"He might have ducked onto another floor somewhere."

"But why? Unless he knows the apartment he's going to, that's not gonna get him anywhere."

"The roof," Haley said. "A bunch of these buildings are tucked close together. He might be jumping from one to another."

Recker agreed. "I'll head up there. You keep going on the street and see if you can catch him landing somewhere."

The two partners split up again. Now Addison had a bigger lead on them. And that was even if they were right on their current assessment, which was not a given. By the time Recker reached the roof, there was no one in sight. He kept running along the rooftop, jumping onto neighboring buildings as he reached them, but Addison appeared to be gone.

Finally, after a few minutes, Recker stopped his pursuit, and looked over the edge of the roof. He was trying to find Addison somewhere on the street level. It was a tall order at this point. He didn't see him anywhere. He hoped Haley was having better luck than he was.

"How are you looking down there?"

"I got nothing," Haley answered. "He could've gone just about anywhere at this point."

Recker slapped his leg in frustration. "Damn! We were so close."

"Well, at least we got his apartment."

"I don't think that's gonna do us much good at this point. He's probably never coming back to it."

"Yeah, but he left in a hurry. That means he might've left something behind."

"True. He didn't have time to pack anything up."

"Let's head back there," Haley said. "See if we can find something that'll lead us to his next stop."

"I don't know about that. But we still have one victim remaining. Maybe we can find something to indicate who he's targeting. If we can, maybe this won't be a loss after all. And we need a victory right now. Even a small one."

24

Recker and Haley went back to Addison's apartment. Some of the wood around the edge of the door was broken off. But they were still able to close it once they went inside. It was a one bedroom, one bathroom apartment, and a small kitchen and living room, so it wasn't a big area to search.

They were hopeful that with Addison leaving in a hurry, he'd have left things behind they could use to aid them in finding him again. After only a few minutes, Haley came out of the bedroom.

"Looks like we hit pay dirt," Haley said, holding up a laptop. "I'm sure David will be able to work wonders with this."

"Hopefully."

Recker continued searching the kitchen, finding some bills on the counter. "This is in someone else's name."

"Now we know how he's been hiding. Not using his real name."

"Question is whether this is someone else working with him or just a name he dreamed up."

"Or a name he stole up."

"Either way, something else to throw into the pot."

They kept looking around the apartment for a little while, until Haley found something else. It was buried under some magazines and newspapers on an end table next to the couch. He sorted through the mess, eventually finding a paper that had a list of names on it.

"Whoa."

"You got something?" Recker asked.

"I think we might have hit the big one."

Recker walked over to his partner and leaned in next to him, looking at the list.

"There's fifteen names on this thing," Haley said.

"Look at the first five. They're already victims."

"And already crossed out."

"That means he's still got ten more to go," Recker said.

"But he only got six pills."

"That we know of. Maybe he got more from a different supplier."

"Or he hasn't gotten the rest yet. Maybe he's splitting things up. Doing a little at a time so as not to draw too much attention from getting too much at once. Or all from the same guy."

"Yeah, possible, I guess."

"There's ten more names on this list," Haley said. "Maybe we need to warn them about what's coming."

Recker nodded. And as much as he didn't like bringing on outside help, he wasn't sure this was a task they could do alone. They couldn't protect ten people at once. And without having any idea about where Addison could strike next, they really had no other choice.

"I think we might need to turn some of this over to the police."

"What? Why?" Haley asked.

"Because this list doesn't look like it's in any type of order, so Addison could hit any of these people next. Even if we split up and take two, that still leaves eight unprotected. I'd rather bring other people in and make sure that these people get the protection and help that they need. If we lose him, we lose him, but at least we'd have saved ten lives in the process."

"Yeah, you're right."

"We can still work on finding him before he gets to any of these people."

"He's still got one pill left right now," Haley said. "Probably means there's one name on this list that's a priority over the others."

"Killing them in batches. The first six he hates the most."

"Which one's that sixth name, though?"

Recker glanced over at the laptop that Haley had

put down on the couch. He pointed to it. "Maybe that'll give us the answers we need."

"Something's gotta."

They spent another half hour going through the apartment one more time, just in case they missed something. They didn't, though. Still, they were happy with what they found. Although they missed the big prize, which Recker was still fuming about, they at least were leaving with more than they came in with. It was something, at least.

On the way out, Recker called Jones, just to let him know what had happened, and they were coming back to the office with some new leads.

"We recovered some things from Addison's apartment, including a laptop."

"Very good," Jones replied. "I can get started on it as soon as you get here."

"Just for the record, how did you know Addison was here to begin with?"

"The phone number that was used to call Mekhi. I was able to use the coordinates to pin down the address, which was the apartment building. I then used some filters to pin down which unit he was in."

"Oh. Nice. I can't believe I lost him. I had him."

"These things happen."

"Yeah, but they're not supposed to happen to me," Recker said.

"You're not superhuman, Michael. To use your

baseball metaphors, you can't bat a thousand every time, right?"

Recker sighed. "No, I suppose not. Still had a chance to wrap this up, and I let him slip away."

"What's done is done. We can't worry about that now. Now we just have to figure out a way to move forward."

Recker and Haley immediately went back to the office and handed the laptop over. Jones instantly opened it.

"Hmm. Password protected."

"That gonna be a problem for you?" Recker asked.

Jones gave him a menacing glance. "A minor inconvenience. It won't be too long."

"Great. Can't wait."

Recker and Haley plopped down on the couch, already a little exhausted from the long day.

"What do you want to do about our other problem?" Jones asked.

"What other problem?" Recker asked.

"T-Bone's killers?"

"Oh. Yeah. That."

"Do you have a plan for it?"

"Well, I mean, I guess first we have to find them."

"That won't be too hard," Jones said.

"Why not?"

"Looks like they're having some kind of party tonight."

"How do you know that?"

"Because these idiots plaster things on their social media like nobody's watching."

"Or because everyone's watching," Recker replied.

"Either way. The one mentioned something about a party with the boys tonight in the parking lot of a nearby playground of one of those apartment complexes. One of the ones T-Bone was previously in charge of."

"Doing a victory dance?" Haley asked.

"Something like that. Likely wanting everyone to know who it was that knocked T-Bone off, and who's now in charge."

"Are the police not watching these guys?"

"I would say no," Jones responded. "If they were, they would have been there the last time they posted something. Either these people are not yet on their radar, or they're spread too thin to do anything about them."

"Sounds like our problem, anyway," Recker said. "They did shoot at us, after all."

"How many people are going to be at this little party?" Haley asked.

Jones' head moved slightly, not having the answer. "Impossible to say. Could be an intimate party of five, or it could be a massive shindig of a hundred."

"Oh. Easy enough."

"One way or another, sounds like a party we should be crashing," Recker said.

Haley looked at his watch. "Do we have a time for this thing?"

"There was no time listed on the post," Jones answered. "It just said tonight. Maybe they have it already pre-planned or something. Or maybe they have a regular time. I don't know."

Haley continued looking at his watch. "So we probably have a few hours to go."

Jones and Recker both looked at him, though Recker already had a good idea what was in his partner's mind. Jones, however, did not.

"Are you in a rush?" Jones asked.

Haley took his eyes off his watch. "Oh. No. No rush. Just wondering."

Recker grinned. "Romeo has a pizza date tonight."

"Oh, no," Jones said. "Really? Are we really doing that?"

"I'm not doing anything!" Haley said.

"I distinctly heard you two talking about eating pizza later," Recker said.

"Yeah, but nothing definite or concrete. Just an idea if there was time."

"Well I think we got time."

"Not if we're crashing this party later."

"Probably got four or five hours until then. Maybe even more. I think there's time for you to grab some pizza with this woman."

"Well, I don't know if..."

"Chris. We got time. Call her, see if she's available

to grab something to eat. Just let her know you've only got an hour or two. Make it two. Depending on when she's available, of course."

"Are we really sure we want to do this?" Jones asked.

"*We're* not doing anything," Recker replied. "Chris is. And yes, he is."

"I don't want it taking away from team time," Haley said.

"It's not. Go. Enjoy yourself for a couple of hours. Get to know this woman. Have fun. This crew will still be there later. Believe me, they're not going anywhere."

"Are we sure this woman's trustworthy?" Jones asked. "She's not going to be waiting there with the police and handcuffs, is she?"

"I kind of doubt it," Recker answered. "She could've done that the last time we met with her. Then they could've had both of us, not just one."

"Good point."

"Stop trying to think of bad things that can happen and reasons why he shouldn't go. It's fine."

"I'm sorry, I'm just a little cautious."

"We know. And that's what makes you you. But this is fine."

"I don't have to go," Haley said.

"Yes, you do," Recker replied. "We don't give orders here, but that's an order. You need to go."

"Well I don't *need* to."

"Yes, you do. You have an interest in her. She has an

interest in you. We're not monks here. You're allowed to have a personal life. Work/life balance. That's what it's all about. Right, David?"

"That's what people tell me," Jones answered.

"Call her. See if she's available."

"You're sure?" Haley asked.

"We're sure," Recker said. "Make the call."

Haley agreed, and took out his phone as he went to the other corner of the room. While he was doing that, Recker and Jones made some small talk, not wanting to listen in to his conversation. After a few minutes, Haley hung up, and came back over to the others.

"So what's the word?" Recker asked.

"Six o'clock," Haley responded. "Told her we've got about two hours."

"She was good with that?"

"More than good. She seemed excited."

"Good. But I don't want you looking at your watch the entire time you're there. If you're half an hour late or something coming back, or if it's nine o'clock, it's really not a big deal. Something tells me these other idiots are still gonna be there."

"Just don't wind up at her house or anything," Jones said.

"Really, David?" Recker said

"I'm just saying. You never know where these things will lead."

"Pretty sure pizza's not getting anyone turned on," Haley said.

"As I said, you never know."

"I'll be careful."

Recker tapped his partner on the arm. "Go have a good time. Enjoy yourself. Relax. Because when you get back, it'll be time to do some party crashing. And hard."

25

Haley walked into the restaurant and looked around. He moved to his right, then saw Cheryl sitting at a booth about halfway down, waving at him. She had a smile on her face as he approached the table. They greeted each other with a quick hug, then both sat down across from each other.

"Glad to see you could actually make it. I have to admit, I was having fears that you might have to cancel at the last minute."

"Nope," Haley replied. "Nothing could tear me away from this pizza."

"I was waiting for you, so I didn't order anything yet. I didn't want to give you a veggie pizza or anything and have you convulse at the sight of it."

Haley laughed. "No, just regular is fine by me. Every now and then I'll get wild and throw some pepperoni on there. And if I'm really living it up, I might put some bacon on it."

Cheryl joined in his laughter. "You strike me as a plain type of guy."

"Well, I do have my moments."

"I don't mean that in a bad way. I just picture you as a meat and potatoes type of guy. Just the basics. Nothing fancy."

"Yeah, I guess that would describe me pretty well."

"I'm pretty much the same way."

Someone came over to take their order.

"I'll just have a Coke and a plain slice," Cheryl said.

"And go with the same, except I'll have two slices."

"Hungry?"

"Busy day," Haley said with a laugh.

"I have a feeling you have a lot of them."

"Sometimes. You probably do, too."

"Yeah, I guess I do. So did you really work for the CIA?"

"Yep. Sure did."

Cheryl kept turning her head as if she were looking for something, then whispered. "Are you able to actually talk about it?"

Haley laughed and leaned forward, also whispering. "Why wouldn't I be?"

"I thought there were, like, secrets and stuff."

"I think you've watched too many spy movies."

"Quite possible."

"They're not watching and listening everywhere, even though it may seem like it."

"I dunno. I've heard a lot of stories."

"And most of them are probably true," Haley said. "I did most of my work in the field, though. So there's probably quite a bit they're doing in the background that I don't know about."

"That sounds pretty exciting. Were you sent all over the world?"

"Yeah, pretty much. It's not really as exciting as it sounds, though. A lot of it's actually pretty boring."

"I'm sure that's not true."

"No, it really is. Because of movies, people have the misconception that ninety percent of your time is dodging bullets and taking out bad guys, and that's really only a small part of it. A lot of time is spent sitting, watching, waiting, talking to sources, trying to find out information, things like that. It's really only a small percentage where there's some action."

"Do you ever miss it?"

"No, not so much. I mean, maybe there was a time when I did, but now, with what I'm doing, there's some similarities to it, so... I'm good with where I'm at now."

"Speaking of where you're at now... I did a little research on you guys."

"Oh? That doesn't sound promising."

"No, I just mean I read up a little on you guys. You two are a little controversial."

"We don't really see it that way," Haley replied. "We

have great respect for law enforcement. They do a great job. But they can't be everywhere. And as much as we all wish it worked well, sometimes the law just doesn't cut it. We're not out there worried about jaywalkers or things like that. We're after really bad guys, who do really bad things, who slip through the cracks. That's our whole mission. We're just trying to prevent bad things from happening to good people."

"I think that's admirable. Risky. But, admirable."

"Plus, with our backgrounds, it's what we're best suited for."

"I can understand that."

"A lot of people wouldn't," Haley said. "Even the police. From what we understand, it's fifty-fifty on who's on our side and who isn't. Some would give us a pass, some would lock us up. Where do you fall in on that?"

"Well, the fact that I'm sitting here should give you some inclination on that. But to expand further, I think most people in life want black and white answers to things. They want clarity. They want something to be definitive. And it rarely is. In my opinion, life is mostly made up of this big gray area that most people live in. Things are rarely this or that. It's mostly things that... depending on one's position or point of view, could be spun a hundred different ways."

"There's probably a lot of truth to that."

"I just try to look at people for who they are. You

seem like the type of person who's trying to do the right thing."

Their order then came, and they dug right in. They tried to leave any further talk about their work in the rearview mirror. Instead, they made small talk about movies, music, books, and other cultural events. They seemed to enjoy each other's company so much that they blew right through the next two hours without even noticing.

Haley looked at his watch. It was five minutes after eight. He glanced at it for a few extra seconds than was necessary.

"Do you have to go?" Cheryl asked.

Haley sighed, while still looking at his watch. "I definitely don't want to."

"But you have to?"

"I really should."

"What's on tonight's schedule?"

"Nothing you need to worry about."

"That's fair. I hope you don't think I'm prying. I don't mean to. I guess I'm just curious about how you do things."

"It's understandable," Haley said. "But the less you know, you'll never have to lie if you're ever in a position where you're questioned. You can't say anything if you don't know anything."

"That makes sense."

Haley kept looking at his watch, debating on how much longer he wanted to stay. He remembered Recker's words, about staying longer if he wanted to. And he did want to. He was enjoying himself. But he was also feeling the pull of taking care of business. And it was a strong pull.

"Is it urgent?" Cheryl asked.

"Huh?"

She smiled. "You keep looking at your watch."

"Oh. Sorry. I'm just debating..."

"On when to leave?"

Haley peered up at her. "Yeah."

"If you have to go, I understand. Really. It's not a problem. I can just go home to my cats."

"Cats?"

"Yeah, I have two. They keep me company."

"I'm more of a dog guy," Haley said. "But I like all animals."

"They're really cute and comfy. They like to curl up on my lap when I'm on the couch watching TV."

"I thought cats were kind of standoffish."

"I guess some can be. Mine aren't, though."

"How old are they?"

"Three. They're very friendly. I'm sure you'd like them if you ever got the chance to meet them."

"I'm sure I would." Haley checked the time again. He couldn't resist the pull any longer. "Well, I guess I should be going."

"Not a problem. It was a nice time."

"Yeah, it was."

"Maybe we could do it again sometime?"

Haley gave her a smile. "Yeah. I'd like that."

"Great. So I guess whenever you have some free time, just call me and let me know?"

"I definitely will."

They got up and left the restaurant. They stood just outside the front door.

"Where are you parked?" Haley asked. "I'll walk you back to your car."

Cheryl pointed to her left. "I'm just down the street. But you don't have to do that if you're in a hurry."

"Not in so much of a hurry that I can't walk you to your car so I know you get back to it safely. I mean, unless you really don't want me to. I don't wanna pressure you or anything."

Cheryl grinned. "No pressure." She motioned with tilting her head to the side in the direction of her car. "Just down here."

As they walked to her car, Cheryl glanced at him a few times. She noticed that Haley's head and eyes were constantly moving. He didn't walk with his head down. His head was up, he was alert, always looking around.

"You always do that?"

"Do what?" Haley asked.

"You look like you're... on high alert."

"Oh. Sorry. Just a habit, I guess. Product of my background and profession, I guess. Never know where trouble's lurking. Always know your surroundings. Look for trouble spots. Know your escape route if that trouble hits."

"It must be exhausting sometimes. Never feeling like you can let your guard down."

Haley shrugged. "It's not really. It's just kind of a mindset. Once you get used to it and do it all the time, you don't really put any extra thought into it. It's just a reflex action."

They finally reached Cheryl's car. They turned to face each other.

"Well, I guess this is it."

"For now," Haley said.

"Like I said earlier, I had a good time. I really would like to see you again sometime."

"So would I. And I mean it."

After a brief silence of awkwardness, the two leaned forward and gave each other a hug.

"So call me whenever's good for you."

"I definitely will," Haley said.

"And whatever you're doing tonight, please be safe."

"I'll do that too."

Cheryl then got in her car. Once she was safely on the road, Haley took out his phone and called his partner.

"All done?" Recker asked.

"Yeah. Ready to get down to business."

"Hope you didn't cut things too short."

"No, I think it was just right."

"Good. Any hiccups or anything?"

"Nope. It was really good pizza."

Recker laughed. "I meant the date."

"I know. No, it was good. I had a good time."

"Good. I'm glad. You deserved it."

"I'm heading back to the office now," Haley said.

"All right. I'll have everything ready by the time you get here. We can leave right after."

"Sounds good. Let's go take these chumps out."

26

Recker and Haley went straight to the outdoor party being held by T-Bone's killers. It was in the back of a small apartment complex, probably not home to more than a hundred residents between the three floors. It didn't take much detective work to find the group. Between basically advertising it on social media, the group also didn't do much to conceal themselves. There was loud music, talking, and laughter. And the group had built themselves a small bonfire.

Recker had parked on the side of the building, where they could still see the festivities, without being too close to it yet.

"Man, these people got some stones on them, don't they?" Haley asked.

"Sure do."

"Right out in the open. Not a care in the world.

Brag about killing people on your socials, then you hold a big party like you just won the lottery."

"Well, as far as they're thinking, they probably have."

"Yeah, I guess so. Still, whatever happened to trying to operate in the shadows."

"These aren't those kinds of people," Recker said.

"No kidding. I just don't understand it."

"They've gotten away with it up to now. As far as they're concerned, why change when you don't have to?"

"I just don't understand the thought process, I guess."

"We come from a different world," Recker replied. "We were trained to not be noticed. This isn't that."

"I know, but... you don't see Vincent operating like this."

"You're trying to make sense of something and put them in a category they're not in yet. These are just a bunch of punks that don't really care about a bigger picture. They're just reveling in the idea of being the big man on campus. It's really nothing more than that. No future ideas, no master plans, none of that. They're only thinking about being on top right now, in the small block of territory. That's as far as it goes for them."

"And it's as far as it's gonna go."

"How many you make out?" Recker asked.

"I see about ten. Twelve?"

"Looked like twelve to me."

"Of course, we don't know if all of them are armed."

"Let's go with the assumption that they are."

"Looks like the original group we're after is all here," Haley said. "The rest must be friends, or girlfriends, or another part of the gang. What are you thinking here?"

"I dunno. Walking right up to them with twelve against two doesn't seem like the greatest idea."

"Not if they're all armed it's not. Divide and conquer?"

"Then you got one going in there against the rest. Still basically the same plan."

"Could just wait them out."

"Yeah, but then there's the possibility of more people showing up. Who's to say this is it?"

Haley looked up at the building. "Hard to believe the people living here just let these people do what they want."

"They're probably scared. You know how it is. They prey on the weak and the elderly. Or if someone does fight back or give them trouble, they make an example out of them to make the others fearful. Probably the whole plan with T-Bone. They showed everyone what they're capable of. They wanted everyone to know who did it. That way, they'd never have a problem with anyone. Everyone would cow in fear and give them a free pass to do whatever they wanted."

"Looks like they're drinking. We could just let them drink themselves to death."

"Some people are more dangerous when they're drinking," Recker said. "No guarantee that'll make it easier for us."

"Well we gotta figure out something. Otherwise this is a wasted trip for us. They're right there in front of us."

"I'm just not liking the odds." Recker continued looking at the surroundings, seeing there wasn't much in the way of cover. "Once the shooting starts, we'll be out there in the open. Not much there to protect ourselves."

Haley also kept looking at the area of the bonfire, which was set up at the back of the parking lot. Next to that was a basketball court that had seen better years. A few empty bottles were being thrown and smashed on the ground.

"I'm guessing the police don't come back here very often."

"I'd say that's a very astute observation," Recker said. "I'm sure they knew what they were doing when they picked this spot. There's also a small wooded area behind them. It's not much, but probably enough for them to scatter and get lost if the police come zipping in here."

"Unless we come in through that area. Sneak in behind them. We'd have the cover of the trees and the night. Might be as good as we're getting."

"Might."

"What's spooking you about this?" Haley asked. "Just the numbers?"

"Well, it's that, and we don't know much about these other people they're hanging with. Plus, there's the fact that we know these people are dangerous. They took out T-Bone and his crew. Two times."

"I'm gonna go out on a limb and say we've gone up against much more dangerous people than them."

"I'm not disputing that. It's the not knowing part that bothers me. And this isn't a contest to see who's tougher or who's got the biggest guns. This is about survival. And I don't want it to be them."

Haley suddenly snapped his fingers, a thought obviously permeating through his brain. "Malloy."

"What about him?"

"He knew T-Bone."

"What, you think he wants to get justice for him or something?" Recker asked. "I'm not sure they were that close."

"Definitely not. But Vincent let T-Bone hang around and operate. He must have done that for a reason. And now this group has changed that. Maybe Vincent isn't so happy about that and this group rising up?"

"So he'd be down for eliminating them?"

Haley shrugged. "Worth a phone call to find out, isn't it?"

Recker wasn't sure it'd be that simple, but he

agreed it was worth a phone call. He took out his phone and dialed Malloy, who picked up right away.

"Hey, is this a social call or business?"

"Business," Recker answered.

"What's the situation?"

"It's in regards to T-Bone."

"Yeah, we've already heard about that."

"Do you know who did it?"

"Yeah, we're plugged in. They'll be dealt with."

"You wanna deal with them now?"

"Something tells me you already have something on your mind."

"Sure do," Recker said. "I'm looking at the group right in front of me."

"You got them in your sights?"

"Right now there's twelve of them. I'm not sure if all twelve are part of the group, or we just got some leeches who latched on to them for some reason."

"And you're figuring on taking them out?"

"That's the plan."

"Why? I wouldn't think revenge for T-Bone was on your radar."

"It's not. It's not about revenge. These people are a danger to society, and they need to be dealt with."

"And it's as simple as that."

"It's just that simple. I wasn't sure what your arrangement was with T-Bone, and whether you'd wanna get in on it."

"There was an arrangement with Vincent. I'll have to run it through the big guy first."

"Make it fast. I'm not sure how long these people will be here."

"I'll get back to you in a few minutes."

"Sounds good."

Recker and Haley continued their watch of the group for another five minutes. Then Recker's phone rang. It was Malloy.

"Looks like it's a go," Malloy said. "I'll bring five or six with me. That should be enough, I think."

"I would think so," Recker replied. He then gave Malloy their address and let him know what the current situation was.

"We can be there in twenty minutes. Let me know if anything changes."

"Will do."

Once Recker put his phone down, he looked at his partner and shrugged. "Guess that solves our problem."

"At least partially," Haley responded.

"Partially."

"Solves the number problem. Doesn't really solve our approach problem."

Recker nodded, agreeing. "If they see a group of eight people approaching, they might start shooting out of instinct."

"But if the two of us approach, we might be able to get close."

"Still puts us in the thick of it once it gets hot and heavy."

Three more people wound up coming to the party in the next few minutes, putting the new number at fifteen. It wasn't enough to really make a difference in any plans Recker and Haley were making. For their purposes, it was basically the same number.

It was about twenty-five minutes before Malloy and his team got to the complex. They parked in the front of the building, while Malloy walked over to Recker's car and hopped in the back seat to go over the plan.

"You guys got an idea about how we're working this yet?" Malloy asked.

Recker pointed to the woods behind the bonfire. "See those woods back there?"

"Yeah."

"Why don't you guys come in through there? When you give us the word that you're ready, we'll get out and start walking to them. We'll try and make ourselves a distraction."

"So they'll be focused on you and won't see us coming."

"That's the plan. Unless you got something different."

"Works for me," Malloy said. "I'll let you know when we're back there."

It took another ten minutes for Malloy and his team to get in place. He brought six men with him. They'd have plenty of firepower to get the job done. He sent Recker a text, letting him know they were in position.

"Looks like it's go time," Recker said.

He and Malloy got out of their vehicle, and slowly started walking toward the group. Once they were clear of the building, and within shouting distance of the group, Recker spoke up to let them know they were there.

"You guys really shouldn't be celebrating."

A hush fell over the group, who abruptly stopped talking and laughing. A couple of them put hands on their guns, anticipating using them soon.

"Who are you?" one of them asked.

"Just a concerned citizen," Recker answered. "But partying and having a good time because you killed T-Bone and his men doesn't seem like the right thing to do, does it?"

A few of them started talking to each other, though Recker couldn't hear what they were whispering about.

"You the police?"

"Like I said, just a concerned citizen."

"Well you better concern your way out of here before you wind up like T-Bone did."

"I assume that's gonna be your final answer?" Recker asked.

"Say what now?!"

"Do you all wanna give yourselves up to the police and admit what you did?"

The laughing amongst all of them told Recker all

he needed to know. Not that he expected anything different. He just felt better that he offered them the chance.

"And what if we don't? What are you gonna do?"

"Well, if you don't, you're not gonna see another sunrise," Recker replied.

There was more laughter amongst the crowd.

"That's pretty funny."

As soon as he said the words, Malloy and his men opened up from the woods, blasting away everyone in sight. It was a little sooner than Recker had expected. He wanted to at least give anyone who wasn't involved in T-Bone's killing the chance to walk away. Now, that wasn't possible.

Recker and Haley took out their guns, though it wasn't really necessary. All the work was done for them. Everyone in the group, all of whom were armed, turned and faced the woods in the hopes of returning fire. None of them paid any attention to Recker or Haley. They weren't the biggest threat at the moment.

The group was quickly mowed down, except for one, who was able to escape from the main pack. Recker and Haley immediately took off after him. The man they were chasing was wounded, one of the bullets hitting him in the leg, though it wasn't a fatal blow. He was losing a little bit of blood, but it wasn't enough to incapacitate him.

They chased the man around the back of the apartment building, eventually coming back to the front.

They were gaining ground on the man, and the guy knew it. He had to do something to keep his pursuers at bay. Anything at this point. He was desperate.

Just as he was reaching a group of parked cars, the man saw a woman about to get into her vehicle. He sprinted over to the cars, as best he could in his current condition, getting to the woman just as she opened her car door. Before she was able to get in, the man lunged at her, grabbing her from behind. He put his arm around her neck and spun her around, giving him some protection from the men who were following him. Or so he thought.

As soon as Recker noticed the man's intentions, he tapped his partner on the arm, wanting him to split out wide. Haley immediately knew the drill and ducked between a couple other cars, crouching down to hide his location.

Recker continued on, pointing his gun at the man, who had his own weapon pointed at the head of the woman he was hiding behind.

"Back off, or her brains are gonna be all over the pavement."

Recker didn't hesitate. "You kill her, and you're as good as dead. Because there'll be nothing to prevent me from killing you."

"I just wanna get out of here, man."

"Let her go."

"Nope. Can't do that. I do that, and you'll shoot."

"What if I give you my word I won't?"

"I don't trust you."

"I guess you got a problem, then," Recker said. "You're not leaving. And you're not hurting her. Looks like you got nowhere to go. And no other options."

The man wasn't backing down yet. But he didn't know what to do. And it showed. He was sweating profusely, and he started looking around, hoping he had some other option he didn't see yet. But he didn't.

Eventually, the man figured he just had to make a move and take his chances. He took his arm off the woman's throat and pushed her in the back. Recker lowered his gun and put his arms out to grab her so she didn't fall.

The man's intentions were to get in the car, though he never noticed that the woman dropped her keys when he initially grabbed her. So he wouldn't have been going anywhere anyway. Unless he intended to hotwire it, which would've taken some time.

But he didn't get that chance. As soon as he pushed the woman forward, he turned to get into the car. But he didn't see Haley on the other side of it, with his gun out, pointed right at him. By the time he saw Haley, it was too late. Haley pulled the trigger, and the man went down.

"You guys good?" Haley asked.

Recker nodded. "Yeah. You all right?" he asked the woman.

"I think so. Just a little shaken."

"It's OK. You're safe now. Go inside and call the police. Let them know what happened."

"Wait, you're not the police?"

"No, we're private security. Go inside and call them."

The woman took off running inside, and Recker and Haley started walking back to their car. As they walked, Recker's phone rang.

"Hey, everything good with you?" Malloy asked.

"Yeah, just had a runner. It's taken care of now."

"Good. With all this racket, I'm sure the police will be here soon. We're taking off."

"Figured as much. Thanks for the assist."

"No problem. Catch ya later."

Recker put his phone back in his pocket.

"Well, that's one problem solved," Haley said.

"Yep. One down. That just leaves one more to go."

27

Haley walked into the office, with Recker and Jones already at their computers. They both turned around to look at him.

"Look who finally came strolling in," Recker joked.

Haley smiled. "Sorry about that."

Recker detected a different look on his friend's face. He couldn't pinpoint what it was. It was just... different somehow.

"You don't look tired and sleepy."

"I'm not," Haley replied. "I'm not late because I overslept or something."

He went over to the coffee machine and poured himself a cup. Recker kept looking at him, trying to figure out what it was he was seeing. He leaned in toward Jones and whispered.

"Do you know what's going on with him?"

Jones briefly glanced at Haley and shrugged. "He

just said he would be a little late this morning. That's all I know."

"What are you two whispering about?" Haley asked.

"Just trying to figure out what your deal is," Recker said.

Haley chuckled. "My deal? I don't have a deal. Everything's good."

Recker was ready to let it go. "There are some bagels and stuff in the fridge if you're hungry."

"I'm good. I ate already."

Recker instantly stopped what he was doing, like a lightbulb went off in his head. He snapped his fingers.

"I got it now."

"Got what?" Haley asked.

"You're not hungry, you ate already, you're late, and you've got a content look on your face. Almost happy-looking."

Haley laughed. "So what's your diagnosis, doctor?"

Recker pointed at him. "You had breakfast with Cheryl this morning, didn't you?"

A boyish-looking grin came over Haley's face. He almost seemed embarrassed to admit it. Jones snapped his head toward Haley, waiting for the answer.

"Um, I may have met someone for breakfast," Haley admitted. "Possibly."

Recker smiled. "I knew it. I knew I could sense something."

"Sounds like things are getting hot and heavy with you two," Jones said.

"Just two dates," Haley replied. "Let's not get carried away, huh?"

"What spurred that on?" Recker asked.

Haley shrugged. "I dunno. After I got home last night, I just sent her a message, asking if she wanted to meet up in the morning. Not sure why. I just did it."

"That's good. Went well?"

"Yeah, I guess so."

"If this progresses further, I do hope you'll use constraint in what you tell her about our operation," Jones said.

"I'm not gonna be giving her the keys to the castle, if that's what you're worried about."

"I just want to make sure. Love has a tendency of making people do wild and crazy things they normally wouldn't. And making them not think clearly."

"Well, we can tone it down a notch on the love talk," Haley said. "We're not there yet. We're just two people going out for pizza and pancakes. I wouldn't exactly describe that as a romance on fire."

"Just use your best judgment on this. That's all I ask."

"Yeah, yeah, we got it, Dad," Recker said. "Make any future plans yet?"

Haley shook his head. "Nothing right now. Just taking it by ear. Now if all the questions are done, maybe we can get on with business?"

Jones put his finger in the air, having something to add. "Speaking of that, did you really need to make such a spectacle of things?"

"What spectacle?" Recker asked.

"Uh, it's a pretty big news story, if you haven't heard."

"No, I haven't heard. I try not to look at the news these days. I figure you'll tell me everything I need to know."

"In that case, I'll tell you. Fifteen people getting gunned down in the back of a parking lot is pretty big news."

Recker lowered his head and put his hand on his forehead, starting to rub it as he prepared himself for the lecture he was sure he was about to hear.

"I mean, we are supposed to try and remain in the shadows, are we not?"

"That's the general idea," Recker answered.

"And you think fifteen bodies is a good way to accomplish that?"

Recker scratched the top of his head. "Well..."

"Not to mention a carjacking?"

"Attempted, if we're being clear."

"And shot and killed right in front of a woman."

"Well I didn't have time to shield her eyes and tuck her into bed first. Things happened quick."

Jones pulled up a website on his computer. The headline was enough to make Recker wince.

Silencer Believed To Be Involved in Mass Killing.

"Doesn't exactly paint a pretty picture, does it?"

Recker stroked his chin. "No, not exactly."

"This was way too high-profile for us. This is the type of thing that can bring heat down. This is not how we operate. This is not how we do business."

Recker wanted to argue or debate the point, but he couldn't. He pretty much agreed with everything his partner was saying. He eventually nodded.

"You're right. You're right. It shouldn't have happened. We should've waited. Should've gotten the group in a more private setting. Something that wouldn't come back to us."

"I know we're all strained because of the Addison thing, but we can't go losing what makes us who we are and what we do."

Recker threw his hands up. "I can't argue. I got wrapped up in just wanting to end it quickly and move on to Addison, instead of thinking about the right way to do things. It's an error on my part."

Jones then looked at their other partner. "And you're not absolved from blame on this either. You're supposed to be there to push back on things if you feel it's getting out of hand. Not just let him go in an obviously wrong direction."

Haley looked down at the floor, ready to take his tongue-lashing. "No arguments from me, either."

"You're both world-class operators, and on this, you acted like a couple of neighborhood bullies trying to knock off the competition. Way too high-profile, way too many bodies, and way too much attention."

"Is this gonna bring law enforcement down on us?"

Jones looked back at his computer. "Right now, I think we're fine. As long as we get back to our usual methods, and stay out of the public eye for a while, this should pass without too much trouble. Aside from the headline, the story does present the picture of how bad the backgrounds of the deceased were."

"That's good, at least."

"But let's not press the issue and give the media anything else to latch onto, huh?"

Recker and Haley both agreed.

"We'll be better," Recker said. "You got my word."

They all put the issue behind them and started working on their remaining problem. William Addison. With it being assured that Addison wouldn't go back to his last apartment, Jones tried getting a fix on where he was heading next. It wasn't so easy, though. With Addison not leaving much of a trail, there wasn't much that Jones could do, other than make some wild guesses. And Jones didn't make guesses or pick things out of the air unless he had some kind of proof or evidence behind it. And it just wasn't there.

About two hours later, they were all on a different computer, trying different angles in finding Addison. Jones was looking up housing. Recker was looking at landscaping companies. And Haley was looking up pool contractors. All in the hopes that they would stumble on William Addison somewhere. It wasn't looking so good, though.

Then, Haley's phone rang. He glanced at the ID, then noticed each of his friends looking at him.

"Wonder who that could be?" Recker asked, a slight smile on his face.

Haley pushed his chair away and stood up as he answered. "Hey, how are you?"

"Um, good, I guess," Cheryl answered. "I'm actually not sure if I'm supposed to keep doing this or something."

"Doing what?"

"Letting you know about things. We didn't really discuss it, so I'm not sure how this is supposed to work."

"I'm not really sure what you're talking about."

"We've got another body."

Haley was silent for a moment. "Same as the others?"

"Exactly. Pulled from the river. Drowned. No visible marks."

"Number six."

"I wasn't sure if you still wanted to know."

"I do. Thanks."

"Do you want to come down and look at it?"

"I'm not sure that'll be necessary," Haley replied. "It's not actually gonna give us anything more than we already have."

"Yeah. I just figured I'd let you know."

"And I appreciate it. Maybe I can repay the favor over the next few days if you're available."

"I'm ready when you are."

As Haley pulled the phone away from his ear after hanging up, his partners already knew what the deal was.

"Number six, huh?" Recker asked.

Haley nodded. "Just came in."

"There goes that angle. Guess we don't have to figure out which name's next on the list."

"I don't know about that. There was what, fifteen names on that list? That still leaves nine more."

"But he's out of pills," Jones said.

"That we know of," Recker responded. "Doesn't mean he hasn't gotten them somewhere else already."

"Maybe we should hit those suppliers again," Haley said.

Recker shook his head, not so sure about that. "I'm not sure that'll get us anywhere. Still feels like we're chasing the tail. Even if someone sold him the pills already, that's not gonna tell us when they're going to be used. We have those other names. Let's sit on them like we said we would."

"Nine names and two people."

"I could take one," Jones said.

"That still leaves six."

Recker thought for a few moments. "Unless we ask Vincent if he can spare a few people."

"As much as I generally like to avoid asking him for

favors, I would have to agree in this instance," Jones replied. "To prevent the loss of more innocent lives, we have to pull out all the stops here. For however long it takes."

"I don't think it'll actually take all that long," Haley said. "These bodies are dropping pretty quickly now."

Recker agreed. "Yeah. It does seem like he's stepped up the timetable."

"Maybe we're making him nervous and he wants to hurry up and get it over with so he can disappear."

"Yeah. Maybe so. We're just gonna have to make sure he's not able to get away with it. If he's feeling the heat, let's turn it up a notch."

28

The team had just finished eating dinner and returned to their computer stations, continuing their fruitless searches. Up to this point, none of them were having much luck in finding Addison. While they were hopeful their luck would change at some point, they sure weren't counting on it. After working for about twenty minutes, Recker got a phone call. He was more than a little curious in wondering what Malloy wanted. As far as he knew, there was nothing on the horizon, unless he was calling about the fallout of the shootout they were all involved in.

"Hey, what's on your mind?" Recker asked.

"Just calling to pass some information on to you."

"Oh? What information?"

"We got a call a little while ago from a guy named Hyatt. You know him?"

"Yeah, we bumped into him a few days ago, I guess. What's his deal?"

"His deal is he wants to talk to you about something," Malloy answered. "Didn't say what it was. Just asked if we could get the message to you. Don't know how he knows we know each other, but..."

"I think I might have mentioned knowing Vincent during our last chat."

"Oh. Anyway, it sounded like it might be important. Don't know if you wanna talk to him or not, but he left a number for you to reach him if you do."

"Yeah, I'll talk to him. What's his number?"

Recker grabbed a notepad and a pen and jotted the number down. After getting off the phone with Malloy, Recker briefly mentioned what was happening to his partners.

"Wonder what that's about?" Haley asked.

"Guess we'll know in a minute," Recker said, dialing the number.

Hyatt picked up after the second ring. "Hello?"

"I understand you wanted to talk to me?"

"Depends on who you are, man. I wanna talk to a lot of people."

"You called Vincent earlier asking for me."

"Oh, yeah! You're that dude. Yeah, I wanted to talk to you. Figured maybe we could do some business, if you know what I mean."

"What kind of business?" Recker asked.

"The kind where we both benefit, know what I'm saying?"

"Vaguely. Why don't you just come out and say what you want?"

"Oh, all right. Well, see it's like this. You were asking about this specific dude the other day, right?"

"William Addison."

"Uh, yeah, yeah. Whatever his name is. And I said I didn't know the guy, right?"

"That's what you said."

"And that was the God's honest truth. It really was. But, uh…"

"But what?"

"Well, you see, that's kind of changed now, you understand?"

"Not really."

Hyatt cleared his throat. "Well let me say it like this, then. This dude contacted me yesterday, asking me for some of those pills you were looking for."

"OK?"

"And so we did a little transaction last night, you know?"

"I guess?"

"Anyway, it goes like this. I didn't know who this guy was when he called. He was asking for a bunch of them pills you were talking about. Six of them. Anyway, I told him I only had three on me. So I'd sell him the three I had, and if he could wait another day for the other three, I'd sell it to him for a bit of a discount."

"And?"

"And he went for it, man. He went for it."

"You already sold him three?" Recker asked.

"Last night. Transaction went down silky smooth."

"Where?"

"One of my usual places, man. Just in a dark alley somewhere. No people, no cameras, none of that jazz."

"And you're sure it's the same guy we were looking for?"

"No doubt," Hyatt replied. "No doubt. His face was the same one that you showed me the picture of. It's him."

"So what are you telling me for?"

"Huh? Don't you want him?"

"Yeah, but you already did the deal, didn't you?"

"No, man, that's what I'm trying to tell you. I was setting him up for you guys. I got all the pills he needs. But I told him I didn't, so he'd come around again tonight. Then if you guys want him, you can do what you do, you know?"

"Seems like a bad business practice for you. Setting up your clients and all."

"Well, see, like you say, it's all just business. Maybe there'd be something in it for me to do this."

Recker shook his head, knowing there'd be a catch in there somewhere. "Which is?"

"I dunno, man, what do you think? Maybe monetary compensation? Maybe some protection rights? Maybe if I'm ever in trouble, I get to call on you for something? Maybe making sure the police don't ever come knocking? Something along those lines."

"Well, we're not gonna be your personal body-guards or anything. And we can't keep the police off you either. Maybe we could work out some money. And maybe if you're ever in trouble with some real bad dudes, we might be able to help out with that. But I'm not talking about you having trouble swinging a deal with a burned-out college kid or something. I'm talking real bad dudes with attitudes. And guns."

"Hey, I would take that. And maybe five thousand dollars, to boot?"

"Three. Take it or leave it."

Hyatt didn't hesitate. "I'll take it. And some protection?"

"One time. And it's gotta be real bad dudes. If you call us and say some old granny's beating you up with her purse, we're walking away and the deal is void."

"Understood, man, understood. Bad dudes only. I got it and I agree totally."

"Looks like we got a deal, then. What's the situation with Addison?"

"I told him I'd meet him same time, same place tonight. He'll bring the cash. I'll bring the pills. Matter's done."

"You're sure he's coming?"

"The bro called me about thirty minutes ago,

making sure I had the goods. I said I did. We agreed to meet tonight. Same spot. Everything's set."

"And he's got no idea what you're planning?" Recker asked.

"How could he? Until just now, I had no idea you were even gonna agree to anything. Didn't tip my hand because I didn't know I had one! This is smooth, man, trust me. You want this guy. I'm giving him to you on a silver platter."

"For three thousand and we scare someone off your back one time?"

"That's it. Knowing I got you in my back pocket once if I ever get into real deep is worth its weight in gold to me."

"All right. Sounds like we got a deal. Where's this gonna take place?"

"Midnight. In an alley between a parking garage and some shops down on 42nd. I'll be waiting for this guy in the middle of it, next to a green dumpster. That's how we did it last night. Same thing tonight. He'll give me the money, I'll give him the pills, and it's a done deal. Won't take more than two minutes, so you gotta be ready to deal."

"We'll be there in plenty of time," Recker said.

"All right, then. Guess I'll be seeing you there."

"One more thing. You won't be seeing us before this takes place, but we'll be there. If anything goes wrong, or you hear from him saying the deal is off, call me back at this number."

"Will do."

"Another thing. Once this deal goes down, if I was you, I'd find the nearest hole to crawl in."

"Expect some shooting?"

"Yeah, I do. And if he knows you're the one that tipped us off, you're going down first."

"No worries about me, man. I am outta there lick-ety-split."

"One more thing," Recker said.

"There's more?"

"This is it. If you get cold feet about this, or decide to play both sides of the fence and tip him off that we're there, there will be no place you can hide from us. Do you understand?"

"No worries, man. You guys scare me more than he does. I'd rather be with you than against you. Don't worry. This will go down easy as pie."

"Well, we'll see about that."

"So it's a go?"

"Yeah. It's a go."

"You bring the money with you?"

"Don't worry about that," Recker replied. "You just do your part. Get him there. Then get out of the way."

"Like I said, that's a part I can play real well. Getting out of the way. I am out."

"All right. Let me know if anything changes between now and tonight. If not, we'll see you there."

"You got it."

After Recker got off the phone, he noticed his

friends staring at him. From what they could overhear, they already knew the basics.

"Looks like Hyatt's bringing him to us."

"Do you think this is on the level?" Jones asked.

"You mean, is Hyatt setting us up?"

"It has to be considered."

"Should be. But I don't think that's a consideration. He's afraid of us. And he's afraid of Vincent. There's no way he's risking bringing the wrath of anyone down on him for this."

"What if he told Addison what's going on, and then Addison told him to do this? Promised him a big payday or something?"

"Is Addison capable of giving him a big payday?"

Jones shrugged. "That's the big question. There are so many unknowns with this man. It's hard to discount anything at the moment."

"So he's basically giving us Addison for three thousand and a favor?" Haley asked.

"That's the size of it," Recker responded.

"Almost sounds too good to be true."

Recker started stroking his chin as he thought more about it. "Yeah. Almost."

29

Recker and Haley were getting ready to leave, but not before they had some last-minute thoughts from Jones.

"Are you still sure about this?"

"We've been over this," Recker answered. "What exactly is bugging you about it?"

"It just seems too easy."

"Sometimes that's how it goes."

"And it seems like the price is too cheap."

Recker couldn't deny that argument. He'd been wrestling with it too, just not voicing it.

"A man like Hyatt, with information like this, I would think he would have asked for a lot more than this. He knows how valuable it is."

"What are you saying?" Recker said. "One save from us from some bad dudes if he gets into trouble isn't valuable."

"It is. But there's no... tangible value assigned to it."

Jones still had more on his mind. He waved his partners to come over to him. He had something to show them.

"Look at this. I pulled up the satellite images of the spot in question."

"Looks like an alley," Recker said. "Like it should."

"Next to a parking garage, which could hold several people who are trying to remain hidden. And on the other side, look at these windows. Up top. Perfect for someone looking down, who hopes to take out whoever is below."

"I guess that's possible."

"And, this green dumpster he talks about? It's right next to a door that leads into the other building. If that's unlocked, they can quite easily escape all the chaos pretty quickly."

Recker rubbed his cheek. "You seem pretty sure that this is a setup."

"Not sure. Just... cautious."

"Well what do you suggest? If we try to clear these buildings first, and there really is something there, Addison's in the wind again long before we get to him."

Haley interjected his thoughts. "And if we do clear them, there's always a possibility that we do it too soon and they get in there after we're done."

"That too."

Jones wasn't backing down from his position. "I just... I don't like putting so much faith into a man like

Hyatt. We barely know him. And what we do know, doesn't really suggest that he's a man we should be trusting in a situation like this."

Recker looked at the time. "Well, we don't have much more time to worry about this. We either go or skip it."

"I think we should skip it. I know. I know. But... as I mentioned, we're putting faith into a man we don't really know. And you know the old saying. If it sounds too good to be true, it probably is."

"So you think Hyatt told Addison about us, and they cooked up this scheme to ambush us?"

Jones nodded. "I think that's a distinct possibility, yes."

"There's nothing to suggest that Addison has a crew or people working with him."

"Doesn't mean he doesn't know people or have friends."

"Hyatt also called Vincent to get us," Haley said. "So in a way, if he crosses us, he's also crossing Vincent. I'm not sure he'd wanna do that."

"Your meeting with him also wasn't the friendliest. He might assume he'll have to deal with you again at some point, or you're a threat, and he might not want to do that again. Maybe he feels this is a better option. I don't know. I'm not saying I'm positive. I'm just saying I feel like there is more than meets the eye here."

Recker looked at his watch again. "I hear you. But we're still out of time."

Recker and Haley finished getting ready, and grabbing all the gear they needed. They made sure they were well armed, just in case things went in a different direction. They bid their partner goodbye and went on their way. As they drove to the meeting location, they continued discussing different options, and quickly settled on something that they thought could work if implemented just right. But it would take some help. Luckily, that help was available.

Once they arrived at the location, they parked around the corner on the next block. They got out of the car and started scouting around, seeing if they could spot anything that was out of the ordinary. They didn't see anything that was strange, though. Everything appeared as it should.

After a few minutes, Recker and Haley split up, as Recker had to go around a few buildings to get to the other side of the alley. They still had a few minutes to go until the meeting time.

"Seeing anything?" Recker asked.

"Not so far. Everything's pretty quiet."

"I'm sure it won't remain that way."

"We're gonna have to time this perfectly. If it's a setup, I mean."

"I know. We just have to trust it'll work out."

They remained out of sight, further up the street,

until the clock struck midnight. They both kept their eyes peeled.

"Hey, I think I got Hyatt here," Haley said. "Looks like he's turning into the alley now."

"Is he alone?"

"From what I can tell."

"No sign of Addison yet," Recker said. He checked the time. "Still have a few minutes."

The time seemed to go fast, as Recker detected a man walking into the alley on his side. It was tough to get a look at his face, though. He had one of those coats that you could pull the collar up, and he had a baseball hat pulled down low.

"I got someone going in. Can't tell if it's Addison, though."

"It's twelve on the dot. It's gotta be him. You wanna move in?"

"Yeah. Just be cautious on the way."

"Will do."

They both hurried to get to the edge of the parking garage. They peeked into the alley, seeing the two men in the center of it, by the dumpster like it was planned. They still waited, though. They weren't barging in just yet. They took a look around, making sure trouble wasn't lurking up behind them. There was still nothing else in sight.

"You ready?" Recker asked.

"Ready when you are."

"Let's go."

Recker and Haley both started walking into the alley. Their eyes were constantly looking around, ready for the other shoe to drop, if it was. Suddenly, the man they assumed to be Addison turned and faced Recker. They were still a good distance apart at this time.

Then, before a word was even spoken, one of the windows to the building next to them was smashed. They all looked up, seeing a man falling onto his death. Recker instantly pulled his gun before Addison had a chance to do the same. He put four rounds into him, and Addison went down.

Hyatt also went down, courtesy of Haley. Then, two more of the windows suddenly shattered, with two more men falling to their deaths once they hit the ground. Recker and Haley looked up at the windows, wondering if there was any more activity coming. It seemed quiet for the moment.

They went over to the fallen bodies, not seeing any bullet holes in any of them. They were definitely alive before they went out the window. None of them still were. They then checked on Hyatt, who was dead now too. Then they checked the last body. Recker knelt down and took the man's hat off. It was William Addison. No doubt about it.

Haley tapped his partner on the shoulder, who stood up, and looked at the windows. A familiar face was standing there, looking down on them.

"Hope I didn't spoil things," Malloy said. "I figured

it was better to be a minute too early than a minute too late."

Recker grinned. "No, I'd say you were right on time. Thanks for the assist."

"Everything good now?"

"I'd say so."

Malloy then gave him a salute, and disappeared.

"It was a good thing you thought of them watching our backs here," Haley said.

"It's a good thing they were available."

"Well, you know Malloy. Never wants to miss a good fight."

Recker chuckled. "Yeah." He then sighed.

"What's the matter?"

"Just feels like a lot of questions we're never gonna get the answers to now."

"You mean how he did it, where he was working, all that?"

"Yeah."

"That's how it goes sometimes," Haley said. "Unfortunately, we can't always wrap everything into a neat little bow. Sometimes it's messy, with a lot of questions we can't find the answers to."

"Yeah, I guess so. It just would've been nice."

"Instead of worrying about that, let's take a victory lap. There's nine more people on that list of his that won't end up in the morgue. And Hyatt, there's a lot of people who won't be getting sold his junk. This is a win."

Recker sighed again. "I guess in the end it is. Came at a big cost, though. Frank, Jamar, all the people on his list... a lot of people got hurt here."

"Well, we did what we could, and saved a lot too. That's all we can do."

They then heard the familiar police sirens that they were all too accustomed to. That was their sign to go.

"Well, that's our cue," Haley said.

"Yeah, let's get out of here."

They jogged back to their car and got in as the sirens got louder. They quickly drove off, a minute or two until the police cars arrived.

"One more case off the books."

"Guess that's good news for you, huh?" Recker asked.

"Why?"

Recker smiled. "Looks like now you might have a few more nights free for your new girlfriend."

"Oh, don't start that now."

Recker laughed. "Maybe we can double-date eventually."

"Feels weird for people like us to do that."

"At some point we have to start living more like normal people, right?"

"Eventually," Haley replied. "But not just yet."

"No, not just yet. We still have work to do. At least for a little while."

ALSO BY MIKE RYAN

Continue reading the Silencer Series with the next book, Crosshairs.

Other Books:

The Nate Thrower Series

The Extractor Series

The Eliminator Series

The Cain Series

The Cari Porter Series

The Brandon Hall Series

The Ghost Series

The Last Job

A Dangerous Man

The Crew

ABOUT THE AUTHOR

Mike Ryan is a USA Today Bestselling Author, and lives in Pennsylvania with his wife, and four children. He's the author of numerous bestselling books. Visit his website at www.mikeryanbooks.com to find out more about his books, and sign up for his newsletter, where you will get exclusive short stories, and never miss a release date. You can also interact with Mike via Facebook, and Instagram.

 facebook.com/mikeryanauthor
instagram.com/mikeryanauthor

Printed in Great Britain
by Amazon